FOLLOWING the Mystery Man

MARY DOWNING HAHN is a children's librarian in Prince Georges County, Maryland, where she enjoys telling stories, making puppets, and visiting schools both as a librarian and as an author. Her work ranges from realistic fiction to contemporary fantasy and has received much critical acclaim

FOLLOWING *the* *Mystery Man*

MARY DOWNING HAHN

AN AVON CAMELOT BOOK

AVON BOOKS
A division of
The Hearst Corporation
1350 Avenue of the Americas
New York, New York 10019

For Beth,
because she asked

FOLLOWING the Mystery Man

CHAPTER · 1

One hot afternoon in August, Angie and I were sitting at the soda fountain in Sweeney's Drugstore, drinking cherry Cokes and watching Mrs. Appleton in the mirror. Following her usual routine, she was ambling up one aisle and down the next, looking as sweet and innocent as a grandmother in a TV commercial.

Pausing to test a few sample lipsticks at the makeup counter, Mrs. Appleton moved on to examine cough medicines, headache pills, and corn removers. After comparing a couple of household cleansers, she came to a full stop in front of the magazine rack. Like a turtle on the lookout for enemies, she bobbed her head to the right and the left. When she was sure no one was watching, she grabbed *People Magazine* and *The National Enquirer* and thrust them into her big L. L. Bean canvas bag. Then she scuttled out of the store with the speed of a snail being chased by a French chef.

Angie giggled and choked on her soda as Mrs. Appleton disappeared into the hot afternoon sunshine. "The little old shoplifter strikes again!"

"Do you know what I think?" I spun around on my stool a couple of times, staring intensely at Angie. Then I pulled the end of my long braid across my upper lip like a mustache and spoke in my best English accent.

"My dear Watson, I believe that Mr. Appleton has a private arrangement with Mr. Sweeney," I intoned. "Every week, he pays for the magazines and whatever else his wife takes so she can continue to lead an exciting existence as a petty thief."

"That's true," Angie agreed, obviously impressed by my deduction. "If you or I tried snitching magazines, we'd get caught the very first time. Mr. Sweeney won't even let us read them unless we pay first."

She slurped up the last of her soda and poked at the ice with her straw, which was why I happened to see the stranger before she did. Nudging her hard with my elbow, I whispered, "Look at the guy who just walked in!"

She glanced at the mirror, then revolved her stool and stared at him directly. Angie will never be a good detective, no matter how hard she tries. She just doesn't know the meaning of subtlety.

"Who is he?" Angie whispered.

"I don't know, but he sure is good looking." I watched the stranger walk to the bulletin board where

Mr. Sweeney lets people post ads for lawn mowers and cars and old TVs they want to sell. He was tall and slim, maybe about thirty, and his jeans and denim jacket were old and weathered. His hair was as dark as mine, he had a full beard, and his mustache curled up on the ends and hid his mouth just as the silver sunglasses he wore hid his eyes. Just looking at him made me feel all shivery. Where had he come from? And what did he want in a poky little town like ours?

"He's coming over here!" Angie sucked some soda up her straw, making a loud slurping sound.

As she tried to recover from her embarrassment, the mystery man sat down right next to me — which wasn't surprising since there were only three stools and Angie and I were occupying the other two — but it sure sent little tingles up and down my arms.

From somewhere in back, Mr. Sweeney's clerk, Richard, appeared. "Can I help you?" He was just as surprised as I was to see an unfamiliar face in the drugstore.

"I'd like a cup of coffee," the stranger said, "and directions to Mrs. Porter's house."

I gasped and Richard grinned. "This little lady can direct you," he said. "Mrs. Porter is her grandmother."

The stranger turned to me, and I saw my reflection in his glasses. "I'm looking for a room," he said. "According to that notice on the bulletin board, your grandmother has a vacancy. Is it still available?"

I nodded, unable to speak, a very unusual problem for me. He had a husky voice and a slight drawl, and he made me feel as if my tongue were tied in knots or something.

As I sat there trying hard to say something, I was aware of Angie. She was leaning so close that I could feel her warm breath on my arm. I glanced at her suspiciously. Sure enough, she was smiling her prettiest smile, the one that has most of the sixth-grade boys and even some of the seventh-grade boys in love with her.

Fluffing her yellow hair, she said, "I'm Angie Wilkins." Since I was still speechless, she added, "And this is my best friend, Madigan Maloney."

"Glad to meet you," the stranger said. "My name is Clint. Clint James." Then he smiled, and his teeth were white and straight and perfect. "Are all the girls in Hilltop as pretty as you two?"

By the time Angie and I had stopped giggling, Clint had finished his coffee and gotten a refill. While he sipped it, we told him everything there was to know about Hilltop — which took about two minutes — but why he wanted to live here, even for a little while, I couldn't figure out. We don't have a mall or a movie theater, we don't have a video arcade, a bowling alley, or a skating rink. There is absolutely nothing to do here, and Angie and I can hardly wait to grow up and move to Washington, D.C., where we plan to open a detective agency and lead exciting lives catching real criminals, not just old-lady shoplifters.

As Richard removed Clint's dishes, staring at him all the while as if he were memorizing every detail of his appearance, Miss Lucas came in. She was my fifth-grade teacher, but even worse, she rents one of the rooms in Grandmother's house and is without a doubt the nosiest woman in the whole world. She has a sharp nose, pointed like a fox's, and her huge eyes never miss anything.

"Well, well, girls," she asked. "Who is this?" From the way she was staring at Clint, I knew she suspected him of being a kidnapper or a serial murderer. She has that kind of mind — always thinking the worst about everybody. Just ask any kid who survived a year in her classroom.

"Why, this is Clint James," I told her. "He wants to rent a room from Grandmother," I added, knowing she wasn't going to like that at all.

"Just for the night?" she asked, baring her tiny, white teeth at Clint.

He shook his head and tried smiling at her. "For a couple of weeks or so, maybe longer. I'm trying to get away from it all, if you known what I mean, ma'am — the big-city rat race, noise and air pollution, rush hour, 'too much getting and spending,' to quote the poet."

His smile had absolutely no effect on Miss Lucas. Nor did his quote from the poet. She just gave him a look icy enough to freeze a person to death. "Mrs. Porter only takes long-term roomers," she said, and she should know, of course, having lived in Grandmother's house since the beginning of recorded history.

Giving up on Miss Lucas, Clint turned to me. "How about giving me some directions to your grandmother's house, Madigan?"

"Better yet," Angie said, fluffing her hair again, "we'll show you. I'm supposed to be home right now."

As Angie and I led Clint up Main Street toward Grandmother's big brick house, people stared at us. I knew they were all wondering who Clint was and where we were taking him. Mrs. Rose actually slowed her car to a stop trying to get a look at him, which was a good thing because if she'd been moving any faster she would have hit Mrs. Appleton, who was gazing at Clint instead of the street.

All the attention made me feel even more excited than I already was, and I found myself hoping hard that Grandmother would let Clint move right in. It seemed to me I'd been waiting all my life for somebody like him to come along. Tall and dark and handsome, just the sort of mysterious stranger gypsy fortune-tellers warn you about.

CHAPTER·2

As we climbed the hill, I wondered if I should tell Clint why Grandmother had a vacancy. If he were superstitious, he might not want to take the room. Before I had a chance to make up my mind, though, Angie started blabbing as usual.

"Do you know why the room you're going to rent is empty?" she asked Clint.

I tried to give her a poke, but she dodged away from me. "Somebody *died* in it," she told Clint, even though he hadn't indicated he was interested in hearing the answer to her question. "And Madigan says it's haunted by his spirit."

"I don't believe in ghosts," Clint drawled.

"Me either," Angie said quickly. "I was just telling you what Madigan told me."

"I never said Mr. Plummer's room was haunted." I

glared at Angie. She might be my best friend, but she doesn't mind making me look bad.

"You told me the room was always cold, even in the summer," Angie said. "You even claimed you heard footsteps in there late at night."

"I did not!" I felt my face getting hot, and I was sure Clint must think I was the biggest idiot he'd ever met.

"It's a nice room," I told him, ignoring Angie's attempt to add a few more embellishments to her ghost story. "And it's on the back of the house, so you can see the mountains from the window."

"It sounds like the kind of place I'm looking for," Clint said. "How about the other roomers? Are they quiet?"

"Well, you already met one of them," I said, making a face to show him what I thought of her. "Miss Lucas. But the other one, Mr. Schumann, is really nice. He's a retired mailman, and he tells jokes and makes everybody laugh. Except Miss Lucas, of course. I don't think she knows what jokes are."

By this time, we had panted our way to the top of the hill. My neck was hot with the damp weight of my hair, and I was afraid to think about my armpits. Since I turned twelve, I've been sweating like a marine, and I was sure my T-shirt was soaked.

"There's our house." I pointed across the street.

Clint looked at the brick walk leading to the big front porch, its wide steps flanked with snowball bushes in full bloom. Grandmother was hard at work weeding the flower garden, and my cat, Holmes, was stretched out on the railing like a panther, his tail twitching as he watched the birds splashing in their bath in the middle of the lawn.

"I live right here," Angie said as her horrible little brothers came running into the front yard wearing camouflage shirts and waving plastic submachine guns. All summer they've been living in a disgusting GI Joe world, probably the result of watching *Rambo* at least a hundred times on their VCR.

"Here comes Badagain Baloney!" Kevin shouted and pointed his gun at me. "Ack ack ack! You're dead, Badagain! You too, Angie!"

"Badagain and Angie. Dead, dead, dead." Sean shot us too. As usual, his shorts were wet in front, and his nose was running.

"Angie?" Mrs. Wilkins opened the screen door. "It's about time you got home. Get in here and help me with dinner."

As the boys ran by, Mrs. Wilkins grabbed them and dragged them inside. "Did you pee in your pants again?" she yelled at Sean as the door slammed behind her.

If I were Angie, I'd have been embarrassed to death, but she's so used to the way her mother and brothers act that nothing they say or do phases her. She just fluffed her hair and smiled at Clint. "It was nice meeting you," she said, pitching her voice so it sounded like her big sister Alice's. "I hope Mrs. Porter rents you that room."

As she ran up her front steps, Clint turned to me. "What did those kids call you?"

I pulled a leaf off Angie's hedge and twirled it round and round, staring at it instead of looking at Clint. "Oh, they call me that to make me mad. You know — Badagain Baloney, it rhymes with Madigan Maloney." I tore the leaf in half and dropped it. "They're such dumb little kids."

"I don't think I've ever known a girl named Madigan." Clint smiled as if he'd been waiting for years to find someone like me. "It sounds real pretty."

"It's my middle name, actually," I told him as we crossed the street. "My first name is Jennifer, but there were two other Jennifers in my grade, so I decided to be called Madigan instead. I think it sounds a lot more interesting than Jennifer, don't you?"

"Definitely," Clint said. "Is it an old family name?"

I nodded. "My grandmother used to be Florence Marie Madigan before she got married. But her whole family sort of died off, so my mother decided to preserve the name by giving it to me."

"Nice idea." Clint paused. We were standing in front of our gate, looking at our house. "Here comes the last of the Madigans now, if I'm not mistaken," he said. "And judging by the look on her face, you better introduce me fast."

Sure enough, Grandmother was striding down the sidewalk toward us, staring at Clint as if he were the Prince of Darkness come to Hilltop to snatch me away. She's fifty-seven years old, but she's tall and strong. If she didn't have gray hair, she could pass for my mother, and nobody in Hilltop ever treats her with anything but respect. Miss Lucas once called her an "institution," and Grandmother acted annoyed, but I think she was actually sort of pleased. After all, it just showed how special she was.

"This is Clint James," I told her before she had a chance to say anything. "He wants to rent Mr. Plummer's old room."

Silently Grandmother surveyed Clint from head to toe, taking in his faded clothes and his shaggy hair and beard. Like Miss Lucas, she didn't seem to be swayed by his dazzling smile. "I don't normally rent to strangers," she said. I could tell by the stiff way she held herself that she was about to say no.

"But he needs a room real bad," I butted in anxiously. I couldn't believe she was going to turn him away, not my mystery man. How would I ever find out his secrets if he left Hilltop?

"Nobody in town is going to rent it," I went on quickly. "Not when they all know Mr. Plummer died in it."

Grandmother gave me a look that clearly meant I was to keep out of the conversation. "How long do you want the room?" she asked Clint. "I don't run a hotel, you know, or one of those fancy bed-and-breakfast places."

"I'm not really sure how long I'll be staying, ma'am." Clint took off his sunglasses, wiped them with a bandana, and dropped them into the top pocket of his jacket. He had the bluest eyes I'd ever seen, and, without the glasses, he looked much younger, almost like a kid scared of getting into trouble. "I can give you a hundred dollars a week, though," he added hesitantly.

I sucked in my breath and picked up Holmes, who was wrapping himself around my legs, starving for attention. I knew Miss Lucas paid twenty-five a week and Mr. Schumann, fifteen. Mr. Plummer had only paid ten. Considering how carefully Grandmother budgeted her money, I was sure an extra hundred dollars a week would really help us. Surely she couldn't afford to say no.

With my heart thumping, I glanced at Grandmother. Her eyes had shifted past Clint, down to the town. I knew what she was thinking; it was too much, way too much, but if he were offering to pay it, how could she turn it down?

When she didn't say anything, Clint added, "I can give you more if that's not enough."

"A hundred's fine." Grandmother jammed her hands in the pockets of her jeans and stared hard at him. She teaches high school English and, like Miss Lucas, she knows how to pierce a person with her eyes. When she looked at me the way she was looking at Clint, I always felt she saw every thought I was thinking and every lie I was planning to tell, so I always told her the truth.

"Money's not the issue here," she said sternly. I felt one thin arm encircle my shoulders and pull me close to her. "I'd like to know a little more about you before I take you under my roof."

Giving me a little squeeze, she said, "Tell me, Mr. James, what's so fascinating about Hilltop, Maryland? I'd think someone your age would want a little more excitement than a town like this has to offer. There certainly aren't any jobs here. Why, almost everybody leaves for Baltimore or Washington the day they graduate from high school."

Clint shuffled his feet like a kid and tried his smile again. "Well, ma'am, this may be a little hard to understand, but I'm in the electronics field, and this past year has just been one thing after another. I've made a lot of money, but I need some time off. You know, to get my head together."

He sighed and made a sweeping gesture that took in the cluster of houses at the bottom of Main Street and the mountains beyond, lying ridge on ridge like dense, blue clouds against the sky. "This seems like the perfect place to get away from it all. Peaceful, quiet, pretty, kind of old-fashioned, like the town where I grew up."

I held my breath while Grandmother pondered Clint's words. I could tell she was relaxing a little. Hadn't she told me often enough when I was bored that when I was her age I'd appreciate not having anything to do? Surely she must be thinking Clint was a real soul mate.

"Tell her what the poet said," I prompted Clint, "the bit about getting and spending." I knew that would impress Grandmother. She knows more about poetry than anybody in the world. Why, she can quote it for all occasions, lines and lines and verses and verses. Sometimes I think she knows every play Shakespeare wrote by heart.

Clint gave her what writers must mean when they say "a rueful smile." "I was just quoting a little Wordsworth to your Miss Lucas," he said. "We met her in the drugstore before we came up here."

" 'The World Is Too Much with Us' ? " Grandmother asked, and Clint nodded. "Do you like poetry?"

"Yes, ma'am. English was my favorite subject in high school." He smiled again, kind of shyly, and I had the feeling he was revealing something he usually kept secret.

Grandmother looked at him, and it seemed to me her eyes were a little softer and there was a smile lurking around the corners of her mouth, just sort of tugging at her lips.

"I have rules, you know," Grandmother said at last. "No loud radio, no noise after ten o'clock, no visitors coming and going at all hours."

"I'm a very quiet person," Clint said. "And I value my own privacy too much to intrude on anybody else's."

Grandmother sighed. "Well, why don't I show you the room? You may not want it after you see it." She released me and led us up the sidewalk. "While you're looking around, I can think it over," she added.

She hadn't quite given in, not yet, but I was feeling

more confident as I followed her and Clint up the porch steps and into the cool hall. In fact, when Clint glanced at me over his shoulder, I grinned and winked, thinking I'd have him right in my own house for the rest of the summer and maybe longer.

CHAPTER · 3

As Grandmother fumbled with the key to Mr. Plummer's empty room, I braced myself. Even though I'd denied it earlier, I was sure the room was haunted. After all, it had been only three months since Mr. Plummer had died in the very bed in which Clint was going to sleep. Surely something of him lingered here.

While I hesitated uneasily in the doorway, Grandmother walked to the window and pulled up the shade, letting in the bright afternoon light and disturbing several flies. To my surprise, I felt nothing but the trapped heat of summer. No chills ran up and down my spine, no goose bumps rose on my skin. It was as if Clint had chased Mr. Plummer away simply by crossing the threshold.

"It's hot up here in the daytime," Grandmother said, struggling to open the window, "but we usually get a nice breeze from the mountains after the sun goes down, and it cools off so you can sleep. You might want a fan, though."

Clint gazed about the room as if he were standing in a museum full of wonderful treasures. "This reminds me of my grandmother's bedroom," he said softly. "When I was a little boy, I spent my summers on her farm, and I always loved taking naps on her bed." He examined the tall headboard and smiled. "The carving's almost the same. Leaves and vines curling all over and something I used to pretend was a fox's face in the middle."

He traced the design lightly with his forefinger, and I stole a glance at Grandmother. Her face was softening, and I could tell she was warming up to Clint as she watched him open the doors of the tall oak wardrobe and poke his head inside, smiling and nodding as if it, too, were something he had once known.

"It has just the smell I remember," he said.

"Camphor," Grandmother said. "To keep moths away."

"It's smells that bring back memories, don't you think?" Clint smiled so warmly that Grandmother couldn't resist smiling back.

"One of my favorite books begins with the smell of madeleines," Grandmother said. "Their fragrance brings back everything in the hero's life."

While Grandmother explained to me that madeleines were a sort of French cookie, Clint walked across the room to examine the bureau, tracing again the carvings on its raised back.

After gazing out the window, he turned to Grandmother. "This is a perfect room, ma'am," he said softly. "I can't tell you how much I hoped I'd find a place like this, a nice little town, a lovely old house, and an understanding woman like yourself."

I cleared my throat, hoping to draw a little attention my way, and Clint winked at me.

"I don't mean to leave Madigan out," he said. "I love having kids around. And cats," he added as Holmes minced up to him and rubbed against his legs, purring loudly as if to say he, for one, had no objections to Clint moving into our house.

"His name is Holmes," I said. "After Sherlock. He follows me everywhere, and he loves to ride on my shoulders." I scooped up Holmes and draped him around my neck like a fur stole. "See?"

"He's a beauty, all right." Clint scratched Holmes behind the ears and made him purr even louder. "Smart, too. You can tell by the way his eyes shine. Like there's a light behind them."

Holmes yawned and showed his sharp teeth and pink tongue. He knew he was beautiful and intelligent. Didn't I tell him often enough?

Clint smiled at Grandmother. "Well, shall I go back down to Main Street and get my van?"

"I suppose so," Grandmother said as if she still weren't convinced she was making the right decision. "Give me a little time to clean up," she added.

Clint and I started downstairs and Grandmother followed. Walking beside Clint, I felt like I was floating down the steps. The most handsome and mysterious man I'd ever seen in my whole life was about to move into our house, and I was going to see him every day and eat dinner with him every night. It would be like having the best father in the world.

For want of anything better to say, I asked Clint about his van. "I didn't know you drove here," I said. "I thought you hiked into town from the mountains or something." That was how I'd seen him, striding into Sweeney's like Paul Bunyan or Johnny Appleseed fresh from the wilderness.

Clint laughed. "I'm parked in front of the drugstore, but I couldn't very well ask you and Angie to ride up here with me. A certain lady would have thought I was the big, bad wolf for sure."

As he spoke, he gestured toward the sidewalk. Miss Lucas was approaching the house, but she paused when she saw Clint in the doorway. Clutching her purse and a paper bag, she nodded stiffly and watched him while he went out the gate, closed it carefully behind him, and walked back down the hill toward town. Then she practically ran up the front steps to find Grandmother.

"What did that man want?" Miss Lucas asked, as if she didn't already know.

"He's taken Mr. Plummer's room." Without really looking at Miss Lucas, Grandmother went on bumping the vacuum cleaner up the steps. You would have thought she rented rooms to mysterious strangers every day.

"Good heavens, Flo, have you lost your mind?" Miss Lucas's eyes opened wide. "You don't know the first thing about him. He could murder us all in our beds or burn the house down."

Grandmother shrugged. "Really, Marie. He looks like a very nice young man to me." She paused. "And he offered me a hundred dollars a week, which is a lot more than anyone else is willing to pay."

Miss Lucas didn't say a word.

"I can't afford to say no to that much money, Marie," Grandmother continued. "If he stays a couple of months, I might be able to save enough to get some work done on the house before it falls down around our ears."

Considering how little rent Miss Lucas pays, I thought that might shut her up, but she just swallowed nervously and started firing more questions at Grandmother.

"Where is he from?" she wanted to know. "What sort of background does he have? Why isn't he working and how can he afford to pay that much?"

Just listening to Miss Lucas made me feel as if I were back in the fifth grade again, but Grandmother didn't even seem flustered.

"Now, Marie, he didn't ask me any questions about you," Grandmother said, "so why should I discuss his private life with you? I'm satisfied with what he told me, and that should be good enough for you."

Miss Lucas drew herself up as tall as a short woman can and turned to me. "You just stay away from him, Madigan. And lock your door at night. I certainly intend to!" Without glancing at Grandmother, she huffed her way up the steps.

"Come on, Madigan," Grandmother said. "Give me some help cleaning Mr. Plummer's room."

When Clint came back, he parked his dusty, old, black van in the little lot behind the house and carried a suitcase and a couple of boxes upstairs. He let me carry a plastic milk crate full of paperback books.

I saw Miss Lucas watching from her window, frowning as usual. I wanted to stick out my tongue, but I didn't. If I got too sassy with her, she might remember catching me and Angie spying on her the day Mr. Walker from the hardware store came to visit her. The only reason she hadn't told Grandmother there and then was because she always claimed to dislike Mr. Walker.

While I was putting Clint's books on the shelves over the desk, Grandmother and Holmes joined us. Holmes leaped on the bed I had just made, stuck one leg up in the air, and started cleaning himself in a most embarrassing way which nobody but me, thank goodness, seemed to notice.

"Mr. James," Grandmother began.

"Please, just call me Clint." He tousled his hair and smiled. "All my friends do, and I'd sure like to think of you folks as friends."

"Clint, then," Grandmother said, returning his smile. "I wanted to make sure you understood that two meals are included in your rent. We have breakfast at eight and dinner at six. If you expect to miss a meal, please let me know the day before."

"That sounds great. I sure have missed home cooking." Clint was wearing his sunglasses again, and I could see the whole room, including Grandmother, Holmes, and me, reflected on their curved surface.

As he opened his suitcase, Grandmother turned to me. "Can't you see Clint has things to do, Madigan? Let's get dinner started."

"But I'm helping him." I pointed to the row of true crime stories I'd lined up neatly in alphabetical order by their titles — *Blood Letters and Bad Men, Fatal Vision, In Cold Blood, Jesse James, The Onion Field,* and so on. I'm a great fan of Agatha Christie myself, but these looked a lot scarier than any of my Miss Marple stories, and I was glad to see a few other books — *The Golden Treasury of Poetry,* a couple of James Cain detective stories, and two or three books on living in the wilderness.

Clint chuckled. "You better go on with your grandmother, Madigan," he said. "I don't want her thinking I'm a bad influence on you."

I felt like arguing, but I couldn't very well tell Grandmother the main reason I wanted to stay was to see as many of Clint's private possessions as possible. She didn't approve of what she called my nosy ways, but how else was I going to discover his secrets?

Disappointed, I followed Grandmother to the kitchen, leaving Holmes to keep my mystery man company. If only cats could talk, I thought, as I picked up an ear of corn and ripped off its husk. What secrets *they* could tell.

CHAPTER·4

After dinner, we were all sitting on the front porch. Miss Lucas was straining her eyes to work on a scarf, one of the hundreds she's knitted over the years; Grandmother was reading a new thriller with a scarier than average cover; Mr. Schumann was telling a long, complicated joke about a man who owned a talking cricket; and I was sitting on the porch railing with Holmes on my lap, watching the sky fade from pink to pale purple and then to gray.

The only thing that made it different from every other nice summer evening was Clint. With his long legs stretched out in front of him, he was sitting beside Mr. Schumann, listening to the joke and laughing at the punch line.

I stole a long, secret look at him, thinking how glad I was that he was here. I'd known all the other people in our house since I was a baby, and I didn't think they had any secrets, at least not any that interested me. But Clint was new, somebody who had seen the world and brought it back to Hilltop with him.

Just as I was thinking I'd scoot a little closer to Clint, he stood up and stretched. "If you folks will excuse me, I think I'll go out for a while." Turning to Grandmother, he added, "I might be back late, but I won't disturb you coming in. I'm very quiet."

"Where are you going?" I wanted to grab him and make him stay, but I knew it wouldn't do any good. Like Holmes, Clint had his own secret life, anybody could tell that.

"Oh, no place special." He smiled and gave my braid a little tweak. "You be a good girl while I'm gone, Madigan. See you tomorrow."

Holding my braid just where his fingers had closed round it, I watched Clint run down the steps as gracefully as Holmes and disappear around the corner of the house. It was dark now, and a little sliver of moon grinned in the sky over Angie's house.

"He's probably a drinker," Miss Lucas said in the sudden silence. "And a lady's man. I bet he's heading for that tavern out on Route 40."

"Maybe you and I should take a spin out there, Marie," Mr. Schumann suggested. "We'd have a great time kicking up our heels. They have a live band, I hear, and the only pizza for miles."

"I would never go to a place like that, and you know it." Miss Lucas held her knitting needles as if she planned to defend herself with them. "The sort of women who frequent taverns, well — " She stopped herself and shot me a look that said such topics were not fit for my ears.

"How about you, then, Madigan?" Mr. Schumann winked at me. "Would you like to go dancing tonight?"

"Of course she wouldn't," Miss Lucas answered for me. "She's only twelve years old."

"Calm down, Marie," Grandmother said. "Can't you see Arnold is teasing you?"

"He won't be satisfied till he gives me a heart attack." Miss Lucas glared at Mr. Schumann, who was lighting his pipe to keep from laughing.

"You can make fun of me if you want," she went on, "but I think there's something very peculiar about Mr. James. He's taken you all in with his smiles and his charming ways, but he hasn't fooled me. I've never trusted handsome men. Especially ones who don't seem to work for a living yet have a lot of money to spend."

"Oh, Marie, you're just disappointed because he didn't invite you to go dancing with him." Mr. Schumann winked at me again, and I snorted through my nose.

"Don't you go getting that child on your side." Miss Lucas frowned at me.

Sensing that she was about to start lecturing me on the way children have deteriorated in manners and morals since she was a girl, I slid off the railing. "I'm going up to my room," I said, giving Grandmother a kiss good-night.

As I passed Mr. Schumann's rocking chair, I bent

down and kissed the top of his bald head. "When I'm sixteen, I'll go dancing with you," I whispered.

By the time I'd taken a bath and gotten into bed, it was almost ten o'clock. Pulling an Agatha Christie mystery out of my bookcase, I started reading, trying to outguess shrewd old Miss Marple. But, as usual, she was way ahead of me; she didn't miss a single clue as the bodies piled up.

Despite the novel's suspense, my attention wandered away from Miss Marple's little English village. What would she have thought of Clint? I wondered. Would she, like Miss Lucas, be suspicious of him? After all, he was a stranger. What did I really know about him? His name. If it was his name. Grandmother hadn't asked to see any identification; after her initial doubts, she'd taken Clint James at his word. He'd never said where he actually came from and he hadn't been very specific about his job or anything else.

Holmes interrupted my musings by hopping up on my chest and using his head to butt my book out of the way. Purring loudly, he insinuated himself between me and Miss Marple.

"What do you think, my dear fellow?" I asked him, peering into his big green eyes. "Is he a trustworthy chap or is he a scoundrel?"

For an answer, Holmes purred loudly and began kneading the blanket with his claws, a habit he had developed as a kitten. As far as my cat was concerned, Clint was definitely a trustworthy chap.

"But he *is* a mystery man," I whispered into

Holmes's velvety ear. "And it's my duty as a future detective to find out as much about him as I can. Right, old boy?"

Holmes rumbled away, on his back now to let me rub his tummy and scratch under his chin. Sleepily, I reached out and switched off the light, then lay still, gazing out my window at the moon, high in the sky with lots of stars to keep it company.

"Do you remember that song Mom used to sing about the moon?" I asked Holmes. "It went like this: 'I see the moon, the moon sees me.'" My voice trailed off because it always made me sad to think about my mother. She died when I was four, and even though I could hardly remember her, I still missed her.

Lifting one of Holmes's paws, I gently stroked the little pads that hid his claws. "Grandmother thinks Mom wouldn't have gotten cancer if my father hadn't left her. Once I heard her tell Miss Lucas that he might as well have put a gun to Mom's head and pulled the trigger."

I shivered a little as I remembered the coldness in Grandmother's voice when she spoke those words. I'd been small enough then to believe my father had actually shot my mother, murdered her. For a couple of years, I thought he must be in jail or maybe even dead, executed in the electric chair. In fact, it wasn't until I told my first-grade teacher how my mother died that Grandmother explained what she'd meant. Cancer, she claimed, could develop after a severe emotional upset such as a broken heart.

When I asked her to tell me more about my father,

27

though, she refused. All she knew, she said, was that he'd married my mother in California and left her before Grandmother had a chance to meet him. "Your mother brought you here to Hilltop when you were a baby," Grandmother said. "She was just devastated, Madigan. And then she got sick, and before I knew it she was gone."

At this point in the story, Grandmother's eyes would fill with tears. "She was my only child," she'd sigh. "It's not natural to see your daughter die before you." Then she'd spring to her feet and find some task to do, and I'd know the subject was closed again.

Since I couldn't get any information about my father from my grandmother, and since my mother, the person who knew him best, was dead, I used to daydream about him all the time — the mystery man of whom no one ever spoke.

Despite the picture Grandmother sketched of him, I secretly convinced myself that my father was the victim of a terrible misunderstanding. Something beyond his control had forced him to desert my mother and me. Maybe he was falsely accused of a crime and had to run and hide. Or he had made an enemy who sought revenge. Or he was a double agent.

The reasons for his desertion were endless, but I was sure he'd come to Hilltop someday to find me, his only daughter. As I imagined it, he'd arrive secretly and watch me. Nobody would know his true identity, not even Grandmother. Then, when he was sure we were ready to forgive him, he'd tell us who he was and explain everything, and we'd all live happily ever after — me, my grandmother, and my father.

Although I thought I'd grown out of having silly daydreams like that, I found myself sitting up and clutching Holmes. "Just suppose," I whispered to the startled cat, "just suppose that *Clint* is my father."

Holmes snaked away from me and shook his ears as if he were sick and tired of being disturbed. Without looking back, he leaped from the foot of my bed to the windowsill and meowed to go out.

Still excited by my idea, I jumped out of bed and followed him. "He could be," I insisted. "I've never seen my father, have I? And neither has Grandmother. We don't even have a *picture* of him."

Ignoring me, Holmes stood up on his hind legs and scratched at the screen. "Meow," he yowled.

"Oh, you." I frowned at Holmes. "Just wait till I tell Angie. *She'll* be interested."

I slid up the window screen, and Holmes sprang down to the porch roof. From its edge, he vanished into the overhanging branches of a pine tree. In a few seconds, he reappeared on the moonlit lawn, ears cocked, tail high, running into the shadows as if he expected to find something wonderful waiting for him.

Wishing I could follow him, I leaned out the window and stared down the hill toward town. All of the stores and most of the houses were dark already, and the streetlights shone on empty sidewalks.

As I watched, Tom Aitcheson sped by the house on his motorcycle, its noise shattering the night's silence.

After it disappeared, I stayed at the window, looking at the moon and wondering where Clint had gone. Not to the Lone Star Tavern. No matter what Miss Lucas thought, Clint wouldn't go to a trashy place like that. He wasn't a drinker or a lady's man either, I was sure.

But could he really be my father? Twisting my braid around my finger, I hoped I wasn't making it all up just because I wanted a father so badly. It wasn't that I was unhappy with Grandmother. She was just like a mother to me, but I still felt like an orphan. I know Miss Lucas always thought of me as one. More than once, I'd heard her refer to me as a poor motherless child.

And the kids in school sometimes said things that made me so angry I'd get into fights with them and have to go to the principal's office. It was mostly Ronnie Orton — he was always telling me I never had a father, not a legal one. "Your mother just got pregnant and lied about being married," he'd say, and then he'd claim that's what his mother and father told him.

Boy, would dumb old Ronnie and his parents be sorry, I thought, if Clint visited our classroom on Parents' Day and gave Mr. Orton a punch in the nose for telling Ronnie all those lies about Mom. Mr. Orton was big and fat, like Ronnie, and I could just see him crashing to the floor, taking a few desks with him. Then Clint and I would simply walk out and leave him there. Maybe we'd leave Hilltop altogether and move to whatever city Clint came from. San

Francisco or Los Angeles, somewhere in California probably.

While the summer insects chirped and cheeped in the dark bushes and trees, I let my memory drift back to the drugstore. Now that I thought about it, Clint had been interested in me the minute Richard told him who I was. He'd talked mostly to me, not Angie, and he'd been puzzled about my name. Maybe he'd been disappointed I'd changed it from Jennifer, the name he and my mother had chosen for me, and I wondered if I should tell everybody to stop calling me Madigan.

He'd asked me a lot of questions at dinner, too; how was I doing in school, what was my favorite subject, what books did I like. A lot of adults ask you those questions, but Clint had really listened to what I said. It seemed to me he wanted to drink up every detail of my life.

And the way he'd tugged my braid and told me to be good — wasn't that just the sort of thing a father would do when he was going out for the evening?

But more than anything else, being my father gave Clint a reason to stay in Hilltop, especially in Grandmother's house. By keeping his true identity a secret, he could get to know me and then, when he was sure I was ready, he could tell me the truth.

As Tom's motorcycle came roaring back again, I crept to bed, but it was a long time before I fell asleep, and even then I dreamed about Clint.

CHAPTER · 5

At the breakfast table the next morning, I studied Clint's face, searching for a family resemblance. Outside of the fact that we both had dark hair, I couldn't in all honesty say I looked like him. His eyes were unusually blue and mine were gray, his skin was tan and mine was fair and freckled, he was tall and lean and I was short and thin. Of course, Grandmother always said I was the spitting image of my mother, but I sometimes thought she simply didn't want to think I'd inherited anything from my father.

When we'd finished eating, Clint lingered at the table, drinking a second cup of coffee and reading the paper. As Grandmother cleared the table, I sat down beside Clint and propped my elbows on the table next to his.

"Which name do you like best?" I tried to sound casual, but my voice came out squeaky. "Jennifer or Madigan?"

Clint looked up from the paper and winked at me. "Madigan," he said. "Jennifers are a dime a dozen, but Madigans — well, they're unique."

"You don't think my father would mind my changing my name, the one he gave me?" Feeling shy, I scooped up Holmes, and he gave me a little cat kiss before turning his attention to the dried egg on Clint's plate.

"Of course he wouldn't mind," Clint said. "Besides, you didn't change your name. You just rearranged it."

I nodded, and Holmes gave me another kiss. "You sweet old cat," I whispered in his ear. "So I should stay Madigan, then?" I asked Clint.

"Definitely." Clint stood up and stretched. "I couldn't have picked a better name for you myself. It suits you to a T."

I watched him leave the room, my heart racing. "I couldn't have picked a better name for you myself," I repeated. Wasn't that almost a confession?

"Madigan," Grandmother called from the kitchen. "What's keeping you? I'm waiting to wash the rest of the dishes."

After I'd carried Clint's plate and cup to the sink, I decided to go over to Angie's, but she'd already arrived at our house. She was sitting on the railing, swinging her legs and talking to Clint, tossing her hair and smiling, acting more and more like her older sister Alice.

"I was just coming to see you," I said to her. I felt kind of irritated to find her sitting on my porch with Clint.

"Well, I wanted to say hi to Clint." Angie gave him one of her new smiles.

I glared at Angie. She was flirting with Clint — anybody could see that — but before I had a chance to say anything, Clint tipped back in his rocker and grinned at me.

"Angie tells me you girls are planning to be detectives when you grow up." From the way he said it, I could tell he was amused at the idea. "There can't be much illegal activity in a little town like Hilltop."

"Oh, you'd be surprised," Angie said. "Mrs. Appleton shoplifts magazines from Sweeney's Drugstore, and Arthur Whipple stole Mr. Rose's car and wrecked it on New Cut Road. Tom Aitcheson grows marijuana in his vegetable garden. And Miss Lucas has a secret boyfriend, Mr. Walker from the hardware store; he meets her in the park and they go off together in his car." Angie stopped, obviously out of breath, and flopped down in a rocker next to Clint.

"Is that all? No bodies buried in the basement or maniacs locked in the attic? No robberies or arson?" Clint laughed. "Not even a counterfeiting ring?"

I shook my head, a little annoyed. I hadn't thought Clint was the kind of adult who made fun of kids. "Once we thought Mr. Arbuckle had killed his wife

34

and buried her in the garden, but it turned out she'd gone to Atlantic City with her sister. To gamble."

"We were right about seeing him burying something in the garden, though." Angie wrinkled her nose. "It was his dog. Arthur Whipple ran over him with Mr. Rose's car."

"We were only ten at the time," I explained. "We're a lot smarter now."

"I can see that." Clint flashed me one of his best smiles, and I could feel my insides turn right over. "Maybe Hilltop's more exciting than I thought," he added.

"It's nothing like *California*." I tried to say this in a meaningful way so he'd realize I suspected his true identity, but Clint didn't seem to notice. Or did he just pretend not to? "Where my *father* lives," I added, still getting no response.

"Yeah," Angie agreed. "It's really boring here."

"You must have seen a thousand towns bigger and more interesting than Hilltop," I persisted.

He nodded. "I've done a lot of traveling."

"How about California? Have you ever been there?" I asked.

"Oh, sure. Lots of times." Clint tilted his rocker back and propped his feet on the railing, so I did the same, stretching my legs as long as they would go.

"San Francisco?" I asked.

He nodded. "Berkeley, Sausalito, Big Sur, Carmel." He turned his head to look at me. "What's so fascinating about California, Madigan?"

"I was born in San Francisco, but my mother

35

brought me here when I was a baby." I narrowed my eyes and added, "My father couldn't come with us at the time, but I'm expecting him to arrive any day."

"I was born right here in Hilltop," Angie interrupted without even noticing what I'd said. I guess she was afraid of being left out of the conversation. "My mother and father were born here too, and they say it's the best place in the whole wide world to live, only I don't know how they can tell. They've never been anywhere else. Not even Baltimore."

"Where's your mother now?" Clint asked me.

He sure was playing his cards close to his chest, I thought. He must know my mother was dead. If not, he was in for a terrible shock. Watching him closely, I said, "She died when I was four years old. Of cancer brought on by a broken heart."

If he hadn't been wearing those silver sunglasses, I might have seen something in his eyes, but, as it was, he didn't give anything away.

"I'm very sorry to hear that, Madigan," was all he said, but his voice had a lot of sadness in it and he gave my hand a little squeeze.

Before he could say more, the screen door opened and Miss Lucas appeared. She was carrying her scarf and her knitting needles, so I knew she meant to settle herself down on the porch and ruin everything.

Clint said hello to her and eased himself out of his rocker. "Well, girls," he said, "I've got some errands to run, but I ought to be back in time for dinner. See you later."

Once more, he gave my braid a little tug and told

me to be good. While I watched him lope down the steps, Angie followed him, her bare feet making no sound. "Can we come with you?" she asked him.

I could feel myself blushing, so I looked away from Clint, out across the green lawn where Holmes was stalking a butterfly by the marigolds. I was hoping he'd say yes, but I didn't want to look too anxious.

"Sorry, Angie, not this time." Clint slipped his hands into the back pockets of his Levi's and walked around the house, his face made a stranger's by his sunglasses. Then we heard the van kick on. As Clint drove past the house, he waved and smiled before he dipped down the hill into town.

"I don't think it's a good idea for you girls to spend so much time with that man," Miss Lucas said as Angie and I started slipping away around the corner of the house.

As soon as we were out of Miss Lucas's sight, I said to Angie, "You shouldn't have told Clint we want to be detectives."

"Why not?"

"Well, for one thing, it sounds kind of babyish," I explained. "And for another, I want to find out as much about him as I can. It'll be harder to follow him now he knows about the detective stuff."

"I never thought of that," Angie said.

"You never do, Angie," I said, trying not to get mad at her.

She sighed and shrugged her shoulders. "Want to walk down Main Street with me?"

"Sure. I have to tell you something." I felt myself

getting excited as Angie followed me through the backyard to the alley behind Grandmother's house.

"Do you remember how I used to pretend my father would come to Hilltop someday in disguise?" I asked Angie when I was sure no one else would hear me.

She nodded. "You thought he was a prince or a king in a far-off land or a spy for the CIA."

"Last night I had a really weird thought, Angie." I picked a blossom off the morning glory vine climbing over the O'Learys' fence and twirled it. "Promise you won't laugh when I tell you."

"I promise." Angie looked at me expectantly. We were standing in the alley now, behind the Roses' garage, and the morning sun was hot on my head and shoulders. Except for a mockingbird singing on the fence, it was very quiet.

"Suppose Clint is my father," I blurted, thinking even as I said it that Angie might laugh despite her promise. "Suppose he's come here in secret to see what I'm like, to make sure I'm all right."

Angie stared at me as if she weren't sure what to say. "Do you really think he is?" she asked finally.

I nodded. Realizing I was shredding the little morning glory blossom to pieces, I dropped what was left of it.

"He *is* kind of mysterious," Angie said slowly. "I was thinking he might be a rock singer or a movie star, taking some time out for a vacation or something. I never thought of him as a father. He just doesn't seem like one."

I knew she was probably thinking of her father, who is fat and bald and grumpy and never does anything but read the paper, watch TV, and mow the lawn. Although he has four kids, Mr. Wilkins manages to ignore all of them unless Angie's mother sics him on them when they're bad. Then he gets out his belt.

"You don't look like Clint," Angie said after scrutinizing me for a few seconds.

"Grandmother's always said I take after my mother." I frowned at Angie. It seemed to me a true friend should agree with you more often than she did. "And his hair's the same color as mine."

"So? Lots of people have dark hair." She tossed her head as if to remind me blondes were much rarer than brunettes.

Ignoring her, I started walking toward Main Street. Little dust clouds squirted up between my bare toes, and the sun had shrunk my shadow to a little, dark spot just under my feet. I wanted to shake Angie till she cried out, "Yes, yes, Clint's your father, I'm sure of it."

"Wait, Madigan." Angie grabbed my arm. "Don't be mad. All I said was he didn't seem like a father."

"Fathers don't have to be fat and bald." I yanked away from her, too mad to let her touch me.

Angie didn't say anything else, but she didn't walk off in a huff either. She just plodded along beside me, chomping on a piece of bubble gum that smelled like grape soda.

Irritating as she sometimes was, I didn't want to get

into a fight with Angie, not today. I just wanted her to agree with me. To convince her, I told her all the things I'd thought about last night.

When I was finished, Angie nodded her head slowly and thoughtfully. "It would explain why he's staying in Hilltop," she said. "This town is so boring, he must have some reason for coming here."

"Then you think he really could be my dad?"

Angie blew a big, pale purple bubble and shrugged. "It's as good a reason as any."

Since that seemed to be all I was going to get out of Angie, I asked her if she had another piece of gum and contented myself trying to blow a bigger bubble than she could.

When we reached Main Street, Angie said, "Let's go see Alice."

I followed her to Greene's Variety Store, where her sister worked.

"Do you see my mother anywhere?" Angie paused before pushing open the door and looked up and down the street.

There was no sign of Mrs. Wilkins or Angie's brothers, which meant it was safe to talk to Alice, the family disgrace. She had run away three years ago when she was only sixteen, but when she came back last fall with the cutest little boy you ever saw, Mr. and Mrs. Wilkins weren't exactly thrilled to see her. For one thing, she wasn't married. For another, she wouldn't tell them anything about Chad's father.

One night they had a terrible screaming, yelling

fight which Grandmother and I heard all the way across the street with the windows closed. Then Alice rented an apartment over Sweeney's Drugstore, got a job at Greene's, and hasn't been home since.

Mr. and Mrs. Wilkins won't speak to Alice, and Angie isn't supposed to have anything to do with her, but she and I visit Alice anyway. We even babysit for Chad when Alice goes out with Tom Aitcheson. Angie thinks the whole situation is very romantic, but, if you ask me, it's pretty depressing. You'd agree if you knew Tom. To quote Miss Lucas, he's not exactly Mister Right.

We found Alice standing behind the notions counter, gazing off toward ladies' lingerie. She looked as sad and beautiful as a golden-haired princess in a tower waiting for a prince to gallop into town and carry her away. Not Tom Aitcheson, but somebody special who would take her far from Hilltop and her boring job.

When Angie and I said hi, Alice looked so startled you'd have thought we'd sneaked up on her and yelled "boo!" Seeing it was just us, she giggled and smoothed her hair.

"You two are just the people I was hoping to see." She leaned over the counter. "Can you babysit for Chad tonight?"

Angie twirled a strand of hair around her finger. "What'll I tell Mom?"

"Madigan's got enough imagination for ten people," Alice said. "Surely she can think of something."

Angie turned to me, but I ignored her. "What's so

important about tonight?" I asked Alice. "Are you going out with Tom?"

"Don't start giving me the third degree, Madigan," Alice said. "Just tell me yes or no." Her voice rose slightly, and a lady browsing at the next counter stared at us.

"What time?" Angie picked up a measuring tape and wrapped it around her waist. "Look, Madigan — twenty-one inches. I've lost a whole half inch."

Alice snatched the tape away and rolled it back up. "Nine o'clock till midnight," she said. "I'll pay you each five dollars."

"How can you afford that?" Angie asked. "You usually give us fifty cents an hour."

"Take it or leave it." Alice turned her attention to straightening a display of embroidery thread.

"Okay." Angie shrugged elaborately. "But I better not get in trouble with Mom. Last time I babysat for you and she found out, I was grounded for a whole week and I had to scrub the mold off the tile in the shower."

"Miss, can you take this for me?" Mrs. Appleton sidled up to Alice, holding out a pincushion, a pair of pinking shears, a plastic rain hat, and three cards of heart-shaped buttons.

"See you tonight," Alice said as she rang up the sale. "And thanks."

After we left Greene's, I asked Angie where she thought Alice was going.

"Probably someplace with Tom."

"I hope not. She can do a lot better than him."

Angie blew a great bubble, the biggest one yet, and then sucked it slowly back into her mouth. "He's not so bad," she said. "I think he's kind of cute, don't you?"

I shook my head. "He's got squinty eyes."

"But he's built," Angie said. "And he has a motorcycle. Alice says it's great riding on it. The wind blows in your face and everything just zips past in a blur."

"My grandmother says he never even finished high school. When she taught him English, he played hookey almost every day."

"So? School's not everything."

"Neither are motorcycles," I said as Angie blew another bubble. This one popped, and for the rest of the way home I watched her picking it off her face and hair.

CHAPTER · 6

Clint was kind of quiet at dinner that evening, but he seemed to be enjoying himself. In fact, he laughed so hard at Mr. Schumann's jokes that he almost choked on his corn. He especially liked the one about the snail who wanted a fast car with S's painted all over it. Naturally Miss Lucas didn't get it.

"The snail wanted everybody to say, 'Look at that S-car go.' " Mr. Schumann repeated the punch line and looked at Miss Lucas expectantly.

"Don't you know the French word for snail?" I asked when she just sat there staring at Mr. Schumann as if she suspected he was telling her a dirty joke.

"Escargot," Clint said helpfully, stressing the pronunciation. "Es-car-go."

We all laughed again, but Miss Lucas frowned and asked Grandmother to pass her the salt. "Of course I know what snail is in French," she said to me. "I just didn't find the joke very amusing."

After that Grandmother changed the subject to the hot summer we were having, and she and Mr. Schumann got into a small argument about the last time it had rained.

While they were talking, Miss Lucas watched Clint working his way through his third ear of corn as if she begrudged every bite he took. I think she was hoping to see him drip butter on his shirt or something, but all she did was catch me feeding some of my broccoli to Holmes. Luckily for me, Grandmother was in a good mood and didn't get mad when Miss Lucas told her.

After dinner, I asked Grandmother about babysitting for Chad. She knew that Angie and I were friends with Alice, and she would never in a million years tell Mrs. Wilkins what was going on. In fact, she thought Mrs. Wilkins was making a big mistake. "That little boy is her only grandson, and she's missing a wonderful opportunity," she'd said more than once.

"I don't like you staying out so late, but I suppose it would be all right, Madigan." Grandmother handed me a platter to dry. "Just don't eat everything in the refrigerator. Food's expensive."

When I went outside, I was surprised to see Clint sitting on the front porch steps, petting Holmes.

"What did you and Angie do with yourselves all day?" He gave me one of his heart-turning-over smiles.

"Not much." I sighed and flopped down next to

him. Across the street, Mr. Wilkins was pushing the lawn mower up and down, kicking toys out of his way and yelling at Kevin and Sean.

"We talked to Angie's sister Alice for a while." I glanced around to make sure Miss Lucas wasn't eavesdropping. "We're babysitting for her little boy tonight, but don't tell anybody."

"Why not?" Clint leaned toward me, suddenly very interested. "Is there a law against it?"

He was staring at me so intensely I felt uncomfortable. "Well, Angie's not allowed to talk to Alice. She ran away a couple of years ago, and then she came home with a baby. The Wilkinses kicked her out and they haven't spoken to her since."

Clint polished his silver sunglasses with the bandana he kept in his back pocket and scowled at Mr. Wilkins's back.

"I know you're not supposed to have a baby if you're not married," I said, "but there must be lots worse things a person can do."

Clint nodded. "You can say that again," he said softly.

"For instance, don't you think it's more awful for somebody to walk out on his wife and never see his baby again?" I didn't dare look at Clint while I waited for him to answer.

"Is that what you father did?" Clint asked, as if he didn't know.

I nodded and gazed at the sky. Little pink fluffball clouds were trailing along the horizon, just above the mountains, and the little moon was coming out over the Wilkinses' roof. It was still smiling, as if it knew every secret on earth worth learning.

"Maybe your dad had a reason for leaving," Clint said. "Did you ever hear his side of the story?"

"I expect he could have told me his side anytime he wanted. He knew where my mother was, but he never wrote or called." I kept my head turned away from him because tears were pricking my eyes. If only Clint would confess right now that he was my father! I just knew I would forgive him. No matter what his excuse was.

"How do you know, Madigan?" Clint asked. "Maybe your mother wouldn't let him see you. Maybe he wanted to real bad."

I drew my knees up against my chest and pressed my forehead against them. "My mother loved me," I said. "She would never have kept my father away from me. Not if he wanted to see me." A tear trickled down my leg, and I rubbed my eyes against my knee. I didn't want Clint to know I was crying.

"Hasn't your grandmother ever told you anything about your father?" he asked softly.

I shook my head. "She won't even let me mention his name without getting mad. She thinks he killed my mother."

"I thought you said your mother died of cancer."

"She did, but my grandmother believes people get cancer when something awful happens to them. My mother loved my father very much, and she was never happy after he left." I looked at him then, but he'd put his glasses on and his eyes were hidden.

"It's a big mistake to keep things secret," Clint said slowly. "Sooner or later, fathers come back and the truth comes out."

"They shouldn't wait too long," I said. "And when they do come, they should say who they are. Right away."

He nodded, but before he could say anything else, Angie ran across the street and up the sidewalk. "Come on, Madigan," she called. "It's time to go!"

"I have to leave too." Clint gave me a friendly pat on the head. "Don't worry too much about your dad, Madigan. Wherever he is, he probably thinks about you a lot. He'll get in touch with you someday, you can bet on it. And think how happy he'll be to find out what a wonderful daughter he has."

Angie and I watched Clint saunter around the house. "I wonder where he's going," Angie said as his van chugged off down Main Street.

"Miss Lucas thinks he goes to the Lone Star Tavern," I said scornfully, sure that Angie would find that idea as dumb as I did.

"Maybe he has a girlfriend, and he meets her there." Angie pulled another pack of bubble gum out of her pocket and offered me a stick.

"Clint doesn't have a girlfriend." I took the gum, but I felt a little seed of annoyance start sprouting again. How can your best friend get on your nerves so often?

"How do you know?" Angie's voice was thick with bubble gum. "He's not that old, and I bet he's a great dancer." She hummed a few lines from a rock song and twirled around, swirling her hair. "Plus he's so cool. I sure wouldn't mind having a boyfriend like him someday."

"He can't have a girlfriend!" I glared at her. "He's my father, I know he is!"

Angie stopped and stared at me. "What's that got to do with it? Divorced fathers always have girlfriends. Don't you know anything?"

"Well, Clint doesn't!"

"Okay, okay." Angie shrugged her shoulders. "What are you getting so upset about?"

I jammed my hands in the pockets of my shorts and strode down the street ahead of her. To tell you the truth, I didn't know why I was so upset. For some reason, I just couldn't stand the thought of Clint dancing with the kind of girls who go to the Lone Star Tavern. Not with my mother buried just a few blocks away in Ivy Hill Cemetery.

CHAPTER · 7

Pausing in front of Sweeney's Drugstore, Angie peered up and down Main Street. When she was sure her parents were nowhere in sight, we ran down the alley and up the rickety flight of steps leading to Alice's apartment at the back of the building.

Alice was sitting on her little porch, waiting for Angie and me and drinking a soda. Chad's diapers hung on a line behind her, and some of his toys were scattered around.

"Where's Chad?" I asked. It wasn't quite dark yet, and I'd expected him to be up when we got there. In fact, I'd been looking forward to playing with him for a while and maybe reading some of his little books to him. He loves me to make funny animals sounds and talk in odd voices.

"He was sleepy, so I put him to bed early," Alice said. She was wearing high-heeled sandals and a blue and white flowered sundress with a full skirt.

Angie scrutinized Alice, her eyes half-closed, as if she were memorizing every detail of her appearance. "You look beautiful," she said.

"Do you really think so?" Alice smoothed her skirt and touched her hair, checking it. She seemed a little doubtful as she waited for her sister to answer.

"I hope I look just like you when I grow up." Angie turned to me. "Don't you think she's beautiful, Madigan?"

I nodded. "Is Tom taking you somewhere special?"

Alice didn't answer me. She just smiled and started down the steps, leaving a trail of perfume behind her.

"Where are you going?" Angie asked.

"Out," Alice said. "I thought that was why you were here. So I could."

"But isn't Tom picking you up?" I leaned over the railing, watching her skirt swirl out as she paused on the bottom step. The last golden rays of the sun slanted across the wall and lit her face and hair.

"There's a bottle of soda for each of you," was all Alice said before she turned and hurried away.

Without saying a word, Angie and I ran through the tiny kitchen and into the living room. We were hoping to see Alice's date waiting for her in front of Sweeney's, but all we saw was her skirt as it vanished around the corner of Tuckerman Street.

"She's not going out with Tom," I said. "He always picks her up here."

For once, Angie agreed with me. "Why's she acting so weird about it? Like it's a big secret or something."

She picked up one of Alice's little glass unicorns and examined its delicate horn. "She could tell us."

"Maybe she doesn't want Tom to find out she has a new boyfriend." I told Angie about seeing Tom roar up and down the street on his motorcycle. "I didn't think much about it at the time," I said, "but he could've been looking for Alice."

"Suppose she's dating Clint?" Angie said.

"You've come up with some pretty dumb ideas lately, you know that?" I glared at Angie. "First you think he's got a girlfriend at the Lone Star, then you think he's dating Alice. Next you'll say he's in love with Miss Lucas."

Angie giggled and put the unicorn back on the high shelf where Alice kept her collection of glass animals. "What would poor Mr. Walker do?"

"Anyway, Clint doesn't even *know* Alice." I was still feeling kind of mad at Angie, but thinking about Clint and Miss Lucas had put me in a better mood.

"When my mother and I were on our way to the Food Barn this afternoon, we drove past Greene's and I saw Clint coming out of there." Angie stared at me for a second, her jaws moving like a cow's as she chewed her gum. "So he could have met her then."

"He could also have met Mrs. Ferris or Miss Malinsky or Anna Grier." I frowned. "They all work there too, you know."

Angie shrugged. "None of them are pretty," she said. "Alice looks like a movie star. You've said so yourself, Madigan."

My chest was getting so tight I thought I was going

to explode. Taking a deep breath to calm down, I said, "Clint is too old for Alice." Too smart, too, I added silently.

Angie sighed. "I thought it would be romantic, that's all." She turned to me, her eyes sparkling. "Just think, if Clint and Alice got married, she'd be your stepmother and Chad would be your baby brother. Wouldn't that be neat?"

"Are you nuts or something?" I didn't have anything against Alice, and I thought Chad was adorable, but couldn't Angie see I wanted Clint to myself? I'd been apart from him for twelve years. Didn't I deserve all his attention for a while?

Collapsing on the lumpy couch Alice had bought at a yard sale, I watched Angie turn on the television and flip the channels, searching for a good show. "Stop," I said, as she paused at a movie. "That's an old Sherlock Holmes film. Let's watch it."

"Okay." Angie sank down next to me as Basil Rathbone, wearing his deerstalker cap and plaid cape, groped his way through a dry-ice fog on the screen. It was *The Hound of the Baskervilles,* my favorite, so we didn't talk till it was over.

"Did you notice Alice's nail polish?" Angie asked as we poured ourselves sodas.

"It was pink, sort of frosty."

"I wonder if she's got any more." Angie tiptoed into the bedroom. I heard her fumble with something in the dark, and then Chad said, "Mommy?"

"No, it's me, Aunt Angie," I heard her coo in this special aunt voice she uses with Chad. It always

53

makes me a little jealous to hear her because I'll never be an aunt. Without a sister or a brother, you can't very well have a niece or a nephew.

"Where Mommy?" Chad sounded a little worried, so I stuck my head in the room and waved at him. He was standing up in his crib next to Alice's bed, gripping the rail with his chubby little hands. His hair fluffed up in dark curls all around his face, and he was wearing pajamas with red and blue trains printed all over them. He looked so cute I had to go over and hug him.

"Get up?" he asked, stretching his arms toward me.

I looked at Angie, who was examining the bottle of nail polish she'd found. She shrugged. "Might as well. He'll cry if we leave him in here."

We went back to the living room, getting Chad a bottle of juice on the way, and sat down to watch the next movie, an old science fiction film about giant ants. While I held Chad, Angie applied polish to each nail on her left hand, pausing every now and then to stretch out her fingers and admire her work.

"Doesn't that look pretty?" she asked.

"Are you sure Alice isn't going to get mad?"

"She probably steals it from Greene's." Angie began working on her right hand, biting her lip and frowning. "Darn, I just can't do it with my left hand. See how it keeps getting on my skin?"

I put Chad on the floor and he toddled over to the corner where Alice kept his toys. "I'll do it for you, and then you help me," I said.

By the time we had finished each other's nails, the

movie was over and Chad was getting cranky. I gave him his bottle, and he threw it at the TV. I gave him a little plastic truck, and he threw it at Angie. When I held him on my lap, he squirmed to get down. When I let him go, he cried to be picked up. He didn't seem nearly as cute as he had a couple of hours ago.

"Maybe he needs to be changed," Angie said. "He feels kind of wet."

"Do you know how?"

"Of course I do. It's easy." She picked up Chad and disappeared into the bedroom. In a few minutes, Chad started crying, and Angie called, "Madigan, come here. He won't let me put his diapers on." She wasn't using her cute aunt voice anymore.

While Angie and I were struggling with Chad, we heard Alice coming up the steps. "Oh, no," Angie whispered. "She's going to kill us."

The screen door slammed shut and Alice's shoes clicked across the kitchen floor. "Angie?" she called.

"We're in the bedroom," Angie called as Alice appeared in the doorway.

"What's going on?" She stared at the messed-up bed and the wet diaper on the pillow and then grabbed Chad out of Angie's arms. "There, there, sweetie, Mommy's here," she crooned to him as he held her around the neck.

"His diapers were wet," Angie said, "and we were changing him."

Alice frowned at us over Chad's curls. "The living room's a wreck. Toys all over, and what's that smell?"

Alice sniffed suspiciously and grabbed Angie's hand. "My new nail polish!" Chad started crying again, and she sent us out of the bedroom.

"I knew she'd get mad," I whispered to Angie as we gathered up Chad's toys and dumped them in the laundry basket.

"I don't think she had a very good time tonight," Angie muttered.

I tossed the last alphabet block into the basket. "She looked like she'd been crying."

"Well," Alice sighed, closing the bedroom door softly behind her, "he's finally asleep."

"We're sorry about the mess," I said. "And the nail polish."

Alice sank down on the couch. Most of her makeup was gone, her hair was tangled, and her dress was wrinkled. She looked tired and sad, and I could tell she wanted us to leave so she could go to bed.

"Here's your money." She handed us each a five-dollar bill. "And thanks."

Angie slipped her pay into her back pocket. "Are we going to have to walk home in the dark?"

"How else do you think you'd get there?" Alice went to the kitchen door with us. "Nobody's going to bother you in a town like this," she added a little more kindly.

We clattered down the steps into the alley. Alice's porch light cast huge shadows on the wall of the hardware store, and Main Street was deserted. As usual, every house was dark, making Hilltop look like a town on "Twilight Zone," the kind people get trapped in when they turn off the interstate to get gas.

As I ran up the hill toward home with Angie beside me, I could almost hear the host of the show saying, "The girl you are watching is Madigan Maloney. Although she doesn't yet realize it, she is about to enter a new dimension. . . . "

CHAPTER · 8

"You're late, Madigan," Grandmother said as I ran up the porch steps. "Didn't Alice arrange for someone to drive you and Angie home?"

I leaned against her, breathing in the sweet smell of the talcum powder she always wore. "Alice was very mysterious tonight," I said. "She wouldn't tell Angie and me where she was going or who she was going with. And she came home by herself. She said nobody would bother us in Hilltop."

"You know I don't like you walking around town this late," Grandmother said. "If Alice asks you to babysit again, you make sure she has someone bring you home."

Holmes rubbed against my legs, purring for attention, so I picked him up. Running my fingers through his soft, thick fur, I looked at Grandmother's face in the moonlight. "Alice seemed very sad when she came home," I said at last. "Do you think she misses Chad's father?"

While I waited for her to answer, I scratched Holmes under the chin till his whole body throbbed with purring. I knew it was risky to bring up the subject of Chad's father, but I wanted to lead Grandmother indirectly into talking about my father.

"Alice has had a hard time," Grandmother said slowly. "It's not easy to raise a child by yourself, especially when you're only nineteen years old."

"She's kind of in the same situation my mother was in, isn't she?" As I stroked Holmes, I realized I felt a sort of kinship with Chad, and I hoped someday his father would return just as mine had. How happy Chad would be. And Alice, too. No more languishing behind the notions counter, no more dates with Tom or trips to the Lone Star Tavern.

"Your mother was married, Madigan," Grandmother said.

"But even if she hadn't been, you wouldn't have kicked her out, you wouldn't have made her work in a dime store."

Grandmother put her arm around me and smiled. "No," she said, "I would never have treated Meg the way the Wilkinses are treating Alice. I loved her too much."

"Suppose my father came back, though. Would you forgive him?"

I felt her arm stiffen around me as if the very

thought of my father chilled her to the bone. "There are limits to my forgiveness," she said.

"But you don't know him," I said. "You've never heard his side of the story. Suppose he couldn't help what happened?"

She seized my arms, and Holmes leaped away, landing on the porch with a small thud, tail twitching. "I know all I want to know about that man, Madigan Maloney," she said fiercely. "If he ever dares come near you, I'll make him very sorry."

"But he's my father. I have a right to know him, and he has a right to know me!" I pulled away from her, angry now. "You're just as bad as Mrs. Wilkins!"

"Don't speak to me like that, Madigan!" Grandmother stood up so fast the rocker whacked back and forth, thumping the porch floor. "A man who would walk out on his wife and his six-month-old baby doesn't deserve any sympathy or forgiveness. Good God, isn't it enough that your mother is dead?"

Before I could say anything, Grandmother swept past me, letting the screen door slam shut behind her. The sudden bang startled Holmes, and, before I could stop him, he bounded down the front steps.

"You better come back here," I called after him, but he had already vanished into the night, leaving me to creep upstairs to my room all alone.

Hours later, I woke up, convinced for a moment that someone was trying to get into my room. Just as I was about to scream, I realized it was Holmes scratching at the window.

Still half asleep, I stumbled out of bed and pulled up the screen. A cool breeze puffed the curtains and made me shiver as Holmes leaped into my arms.

"Where have you been, you wicked creature?" I peered into his green eyes, but they gave away nothing.

Batting my nose lightly with a velvety smooth paw, Holmes purred his contentment. Then he yawned, reminding me that it was very late, probably nearly dawn.

As I turned away from the window, I heard Clint's van approaching the house. I watched him turn off the lights and the engine, coast silently into the driveway, and vanish around the side of the house.

Knowing he couldn't see me, I waited for him to reappear under my window, shimmering like a man made of starlight and shadows. While I watched him, he paused and gazed across the street at the Wilkinses' house and beyond at the mountains, barely visible against the pale sky. Then he tiptoed silently up the front steps, his head bent, his hair silvered by the moon.

How like Holmes he was, I thought, as I listened to his light step in the hall and the almost soundless turning of his key. Full of mysteries and secrets, roaming the night and coming home at dawn.

"Where have you been?" I whispered to the darkness. "And what were you doing?" But I knew I'd get no more of an answer from Clint than I'd get from Holmes. Not till he was ready. Then he'd tell me everything, I was sure of it.

The next time I saw Clint, the sun was shining and I was sitting on the front porch shelling peas for dinner.

"What are you up to, Madigan?" Clint asked as he lowered himself into the chair next to me. He'd been gone all day, and I'd missed seeing him at breakfast.

My heart went bippety bip when he smiled, and I held out the bowl. "I'm fixing these. Want to help?"

Clint laughed and took a handful of pods. While I watched the peas fly into the bowl, he told me about his fishing trip. "I caught a nice mess of trout this afternoon, and your grandmother's fixing them for dinner tonight."

He leaned back in the rocker and propped his feet on the railing, something Grandmother always tells me not to do. "Nothing tastes better than fresh fish."

"I wish I could go fishing," I said suddenly.

"I didn't know girls liked that kind of stuff." Clint smiled at me. He was wearing his silver sunglasses, and I could see two little reflections of me sitting on the porch with the bowl of peas in my lap.

"Before he got sick, Mr. Plummer used to take Angie and me fishing at Greenwood Lake," I told him. "It's real pretty, and you can swim there too." Then I sighed. "We haven't been to Greenwood all summer."

"Doesn't your Grandmother ever take you?"

"She's too busy." I popped a bunch of peas out of the pod. Grandmother and I had barely spoken a word to each other all day, thanks to our conversation last night. "She's got gardening and housework and cooking to do, plus stuff for school. Lesson plans and boring things like that."

"Well, now," Clint said slowly, "do you think she'd let me take you and Angie to Greenwood Lake one day?"

"Do you mean it?" I was so amazed, I could hardly speak. It was just what I'd been hoping he'd say, but you know how it is with stuff like that. Rarely does anybody ever take the hint and say just what you want them to.

"Of course I mean it." Clint handed the bowl of peas back to me. "We can go tomorrow if the weather's nice."

I jumped out of my chair, resisting the urge to hug him, and ran down the hall to the kitchen.

"Are those peas ready?" Grandmother looked up from a pile of fish fillets, knife in hand. Her tone of voice told me she was now in a neutral mood as far as I was concerned. A little cool, but not mad any more.

I put the bowl down on the counter, trying to avoid looking at the fish bones and innards lying in a bloody heap on the sink drainboard. "I was telling Clint about Greenwood Lake," I said casually, "and he wants to know if he can take Angie and me there tomorrow. You know, like Mr. Plummer used to."

When Grandmother didn't answer right away, I glanced across the kitchen at her. She was flouring the fish, her head bent so I couldn't see her face. "I guess it would be all right," she said at last, "as long as you're not gone too long."

Forgiving her for everything, I ran to her side and

gave her a big hug to thank her. "Isn't Clint the nicest person?" I asked her.

She nodded and pushed me gently away. "Oh, look at you," she said. "I got flour all over your T-shirt."

"Aren't you glad you rented him a room?" I brushed her white handprints off my shirt.

"Things seem to be working out all right." Grandmother lifted a lid to check the corn and then dropped a fish into the skillet. It sizzled in the hot oil, and I jumped back as a drop hit my arm.

"Just all right?" I spun around the table, almost tripping over Holmes, and danced out the door. "It's just wonderful," I called to Grandmother from the hallway. "Just plain wonderful!"

CHAPTER·9

As soon as dinner was over, I ran across the street to Angie's house and rang the doorbell. Through the screen, I could see Mr. Wilkins sitting in his recliner chair, a can of beer on the floor beside him. The television was blasting the local news, but Mr. Wilkins was sleeping right through a report on a series of burglaries in Mount Pleasant. From somewhere in the back of the house, Mrs. Wilkins yelled, "Come in!" and I dashed upstairs to Angie's room.

Angie was sprawled on her bed, her feet on the wall, listening to "Country Swing," one of her favorite radio programs. "Isn't this a great song?" she yelled.

Ignoring the music blaring at me, I bounced down beside her, tumbling a row of teddy bears and dolls off the bed. "Guess what?" I shouted to make myself heard.

Angie started to tell me to shut up, but when she heard about Clint taking us to Greenwood Lake, she jumped up and down, shouting, "Neat-o!"

"Come on," she said. "Let's go ask Mom!"

Mrs. Wilkins was sitting at the kitchen table, smoking a cigarette and reading a thick paperback romance, the kind Grandmother snorts at. "Lusty busties," she calls them.

When she saw us, Mrs. Wilkins frowned, and my heart sank. She was going to say no, I just knew it. Probably because we'd interrupted her in the middle of a big love scene.

"Absolutely not," she said, just as I thought she would, before Angie was even finished talking.

"Why?" Angie whined. "Madigan can go!"

"If Flo Porter wants to trust every drifter passing through Hilltop, that's her problem." Mrs. Wilkins said this as if I were across the street instead of standing right next to her. "No daughter of mine is going anywhere with a stranger."

"Clint's not a stranger," Angie protested. "He lives in Madigan's house!"

"He rents a room," Mrs. Wilkins said coldly. "Mrs. Porter doesn't know a thing about him. He could disappear tomorrow."

She took a deep drag on her cigarette and scowled at us both through the cloud of smoke she exhaled. "The less you girls have to do with him, the better."

Angie rolled her eyes at me. "I'll ask Daddy, then! I bet he'll say yes."

Angie ran into the living room with me at her heels.

Boy, I thought, wait till Mrs. Wilkins finds out who Clint is. She'll really feel stupid.

Mr. Wilkins didn't like the idea any better than Mrs. Wilkins did. "Forget it," he said. "You're not going anywhere with some guy in a van."

"Bang, bang, you're dead, Badagain!" Kevin shouted as he ran through the living room.

"You!" Mr. Wilson shoved himself up and out of his chair and went after Kevin. "What do you think this is, a war zone?"

I followed Angie outside, but not fast enough to miss hearing Kevin get a few well-deserved whacks on the rear end.

Heaving a great sigh, Angie sat down on the porch steps. "See what I mean about fathers?" she asked me. "You should be glad you don't have one."

To avoid answering her, I scratched a mosquito bite. Of course I wouldn't want a father like Mr. Wilkins. But I didn't have one. I had Clint. Tall, handsome Clint, the most perfect father in the whole wide world.

"You could at least act like you're sorry I'm not going." Angie gave me a hard poke in the side. "I don't think you even care. You just want Clint all to yourself!"

"Don't be silly." I edged away from her, not wanting another sharp dig. She was letting her nails grow, and they were already almost as long as Alice's.

"Clint's not your father," she said abruptly. "I just know he's not!"

"You don't know anything!" Suddenly I was glad

Angie wasn't going to Greenwood Lake with Clint and me. I could just see her. She'd probably wear her bikini and blow bubbles and flirt with him the whole time.

"Clint's not old enough to be your father," Angie went on even though I was ignoring her. "He's only twenty-five, and you're twelve. Nobody's a father when they're thirteen!"

"How do you know how old Clint is?" I tried to sound as scornful as one of those women in the soap operas Angie loves to watch.

"My mom said so, and she's good at guessing ages." Angie tossed her hair and smirked at me.

"Well, she's wrong," I told her. "Grandmother says he's thirty-five if he's a day, and that makes him just right because he and my mom got married when they were in college."

We stood there glaring at each other for a few minutes. The light in Angie's living room streamed out the front door, illuminating the edges of her hair and making it hard to see her face. In the yard, Kevin and Sean were chasing lightning bugs, trying to fill a jar with them. Through their yelling, Angie said, "Let's not fight, Madigan."

"I wasn't fighting," I said, feeling sulky. "You started it."

"I'm just mad, that's all." She sighed. "My parents are so dumb sometimes. They think I'm going to turn out like Alice. You know, run off and get pregnant or something. That's why they never let me do anything."

I swatted a mosquito, then licked my finger to wipe away the smear of blood it left. "Do you really think Clint isn't my father?"

Angie shrugged. "Oh, I don't know, Madigan. I don't know." She put her head down on her knees as if she were tired of thinking about Clint.

"Everything gets on my nerves," she muttered. "My parents and all their stupid rules. Kevin and Sean. This town, I just wish the years would hurry up and go past and I'd be grown up and free to do whatever I want."

I didn't say anything, but it seemed to me that you grew up fast enough whether you wanted to or not, and you stayed grown up a long, long time. And, from what I'd seen, most adults spent their days doing things I certainly didn't want to do — housecleaning, cooking, working. What kind of freedom was that?

Clint and Clint alone seemed to have the kind of life Angie was talking about.

While I was trying to think of a way to tell Angie this, I heard Grandmother calling me. "I have to go home," I told Angie, thinking I'd argue with her some other time when she was in a better mood. I hesitated on the edge of the light cast by the lamp in the living room window.

"I really wish you were coming with Clint and me tomorrow," I said hesitantly.

"Me, too," she said before she turned and ran inside.

CHAPTER · 10

At ten o'clock the next morning, I followed Clint to his van and climbed in beside him. I was wearing a T-shirt over my bathing suit, and I was carrying the fishing rod Mr. Plummer had given me last summer. As excited as I was, though, I felt sorry for Angie when I saw her standing on her front porch watching us go by. I waved to her, but she looked so depressed you'd have thought the van was a hearse carrying away the bodies of her nearest and dearest.

"Why wouldn't Angie's mother let her come?" Clint asked.

I fiddled with the end of my braid, feeling a little embarrassed. "Well, her mother doesn't know you," I said at last.

Clint glanced at me and smiled. "She doesn't trust me, does she?"

"If she knew you better, she would."

For some reason, Clint thought that was a very funny answer. He didn't stop chuckling till we drove past Greene's Variety Store.

"There's Angie's sister, Alice." I pointed her out as she vanished into the store. "The one I was telling you about."

Clint didn't say anything, but I was sure the eyes behind those silver glasses had taken a good look at Alice.

"Do you think she's pretty?" I asked.

Without looking at me, Clint shrugged. "She's okay, I guess."

I leaned back in the seat and put my bare feet on the dashboard, glad he wasn't overly impressed with Alice. "Tom Aitcheson, the guy who grows pot in his vegetable garden, is crazy about her," I told Clint, "but she doesn't like him as much as she used to. In fact, Angie and I think she's met somebody else."

I watched Clint's face closely as I told him about Alice, and I thought I saw a little muscle twitch in his cheek. "She deserves somebody a whole lot better than Tom," I added when he didn't say anything.

"Maybe she's waiting for Chad's father to come back," Clint said.

"Well, he's taking his time, isn't he?" I looked out the window and wished Miss Lucas could see me riding through town in Clint's van. Would she ever have something to talk about!

"Alice seems to be holding up pretty well," Clint

said as we started up the hill leading out of town. "She looks healthy. No sign of a broken heart or cancer."

"She probably didn't love Chad's daddy as much as my mother loved my father." I frowned at him, thinking he had no business to joke about my mother's death. After all, it was his fault she was buried in Ivy Hill Cemetery instead of sitting next to him at this very minute.

"Oh, I don't know about that, Madigan." Clint gave my braid a little tug and smiled at me. "Do you think Chad misses his daddy?"

"Of course not. He's too little."

"When he's a little older, maybe you and Chad could start a missing father's club."

"That's not very funny," I said. "Sometimes I think my father's not missing at all. He could be right here in this very town, keeping his identity a secret."

"Why would he do that?" Clint sounded puzzled.

"Maybe he thinks I hate him for leaving me, but I don't. No matter what Grandmother says, I'm sure he had a good reason for walking out."

"Like the government sent him on a secret mission or something?"

I nodded. "If he's here, I wish he'd tell me." I stared long and hard at Clint, but all he did was turn on the radio and play with the tuner till he got Hank Williams singing "Your Cheatin' Heart."

By this time we were about to leave the town behind, but just as I was starting to tell Clint which way to go, a police car pulled onto the road ahead of us.

72

To my surprise, Clint slowed down and turned off onto a side street. "Who lives in these big old houses?" he asked.

"This is Locust Hill," I told him, "where all the rich people live. But you should have stayed on Route 12. Greenwood Lake was straight ahead."

"I just wanted to get a look at these places." Clint drove slowly down Locust Avenue. "I like Victorian architecture, don't you?"

I shrugged. "Most of the people here are snobs. Julie Piranesi, for instance. She lives there." I pointed at Julie's house, a big white one with a cupola on the roof and a tower on the side and lots of stained glass windows. "Her father's a doctor, and they're loaded. All Julie does is brag. According to her, they have five TVs and three VCRs and two or three computers, plus her mother's antique doll collection. Angie and I hate her."

"She has a swimming pool in the backyard." Clint was staring at the house the way Holmes watches a mouse hole. "Maybe we should stop and ask her if we could take a dip."

"Even if Julie were home she'd say no, but she's in Ocean City. Her family has a condominium right on the beach." I sighed to show him what I thought of people who owned condominiums in Ocean City but wouldn't even invite someone like me to swim in their pool.

"How about that house? The big brick one with green shutters. Who lives there?"

"The Griffins. He runs the only funeral parlor in

Hilltop, so he's loaded too. Grandmother says Doctor Piranesi sends him all his failures."

"You must know everyone in Hilltop," Clint said.

"I do." I smiled at him. "I can tell you about every single person in Locust Hill or anywhere else in this town."

To prove it, I pointed out all the houses we passed and told Clint about the people who lived in them. Then we drove back to Route 12 and headed out to Greenwood Lake.

It was a wonderful summer day, hot in the sun and cool in the shade, and the sky was as blue as Clint's eyes. I felt so proud walking down the dock beside him, and I hoped the old man in charge of the boats would say something about us looking alike. He didn't, but it was all right anyway because he said, "You make sure your daughter keeps that life jacket on," and Clint didn't correct him. He just nodded his head and murmured, "You heard what the man said, Madigan."

Clint rowed our little boat down the lake, away from the swimming area, and we fished for a couple of hours. All we caught were sunfish, none of which were big enough to keep, but it was fun to feel them nibble at the bait and to pull them in, hoping each time we'd caught a big one.

"I don't know about you, Madigan," Clint said after a while, "but I think I've had enough sun for today. Let's find a shady place and eat lunch."

He let me row toward a little cove. I'm pretty bad

at handling oars, and I kept splashing water into the boat, but Clint didn't get mad; he just laughed, the way I always imagined a father would. When we were about ten feet from shore, he took the oars again, and I jumped into the water and swam beside the boat. It was a great way to cool off.

Grandmother had packed us a big lunch — fried chicken, tomatoes from her garden, pickles, rolls, chocolate cake, and a thermos full of icy-cold lemonade. After we'd eaten, we lay on our backs under the trees and watched the clouds shift shapes as they drifted past. Clint pointed out an elephant thinning itself into an alligator, and I showed him a whale breaking up into a flock of sheep and then floating away like wisps of white cotton against the deep-blue sky.

After watching a dragon change slowly into a bear with a couple of cubs high overhead, I glanced at Clint. He was half asleep, probably because he'd been out late again last night, and I decided to catch him unawares with some questions.

"Where did you live before you came to Hilltop?" To hide my eagerness to know all about him, I kept my eyes on the clouds and tried to sound casual.

"Over the hills and far away," Clint drawled.

"No, really." I plucked a blade of grass and chewed on the sweet end of it. "Where did you come from?"

"Oh, here and there." He sat up and pulled a harmonica out of his pocket. "Mostly there."

Before I could ask another question, he started playing "Down in the Valley" real slow and sad. It made me feel lonesome just listening to him. Lonesome for places I'd never been, lonesome for people I'd never met.

He paused a minute. "Can you sing, Madigan?"

I tossed the grass away, and then, while he played, I sang all the old songs we knew — "She'll Be Comin' Round the Mountain," "I Been Workin' on the Railroad," "Sixteen Miles on the Erie Canal," "Shenandoah," "My Darlin' Clementine." If I forgot the words, I made up new ones that made us both laugh.

"You sure play well," I told Clint when he finally wiped the harmonica with his bandana and dropped it in his pocket.

He thanked me, and we drank some lemonade. When Clint stretched out again on the grass, I decided to ask another question. "What did you do before you came here?"

"Oh, nothing much," he said lazily. "Just bummed around the country playing my harmonica."

"Seriously, Clint." I tried to sound stern.

"Seriously?" He smiled. "I was getting my Ph.D. in the school of hard knocks."

"You told my Grandmother you were in the electronics business," I reminded him.

He laughed. "I thought you wanted to hear something more exciting than the truth, Madigan Maloney."

I shook my head so hard my braid thumped against my shoulders. "I want to know the truth, the whole truth, and nothing but the truth. I want to know everything about you. When you were born, what you were like when you were little, all the places you've been and the people you've known."

"My life history?"

"Yes, complete and unabridged." I leaned toward him, gazing into his eyes. "For instance," I said, "have you ever been married?"

"Oh, once or twice."

"Once or twice?" I stared at him. As usual, he'd surprised *me*. "Don't you know for sure?"

His eyes were the same blue as the sky and just as deep. "It was a long time ago."

"Are you very old, then?"

"Thirty-three," he said slowly, as if he had to stop and think about it. "The first time I got married, I was only twenty. Then I tried it again, but I was still too young. Now I think I'll stay a bachelor."

"Do you have any children?"

He chuckled. "What is this — twenty questions?"

"I just want to know, that's all."

"Well, if I did, I'd want a daughter just like you." He got to his feet and stretched.

"The man at the boat place thought I *was* your daughter." I squinted up at him, too blinded by the sun to see his face clearly. Why couldn't he just tell me? Why did he keep teasing me?

"It's after three already, Madigan, and I promised your grandmother I'd have you home by four. We'd better get going." Turning away from me, Clint started loading our things into the boat. When everything was on board, he held out his hand to steady me and helped me to climb in.

As Clint rowed slowly back to the dock, I sat quietly in the stern, watching our picnic place shrink in the distance. The sun sparkled on the water, and a little breeze toyed with my hair, but a shadow had fallen on the day. Glimpsing a heron standing as still as driftwood near the shore, I pointed it out to Clint, but he barely glanced at it. He was a stranger again, his eyes hidden behind his silver glasses.

"Are you mad at me?" I asked as we tossed our stuff into the back of the van.

"Why would I be mad?" Clint asked.

"Maybe I was asking too many questions." I climbed into the van next to him and pulled my shirt on over my bathing suit. My chest felt tight, and I wished I hadn't been so nosy. I'd probably made such a pest of myself he didn't want me to be his daughter anymore.

Clint laughed and tweaked my braid. "You can ask all the questions you like, Madigan. Don't get mad, though, if I don't answer them." He started the van and we pulled out of the parking lot. "I'm a very private person."

I turned my head to watch the last glimmer of water disappear behind the trees. Then I said, "I'm glad you're not mad, because I had a good time today."

"Well, I had a good time too." He smiled at me. "Maybe next time we'll even catch some fish."

That evening, I went over to Angie's. As soon as we'd settled ourselves on her back steps, I told her about my day at the lake with Clint. "But he didn't say anything about being my father," I said sadly. "In fact, he wouldn't answer me when I asked him if he had any children. He said I could ask all the questions I wanted, but he didn't have to answer them."

Angie blew a bubble, popped it loudly, and sucked it back into her mouth. "I just wish you'd quit worrying about it," she said. "It's all you ever think about."

"Maybe there's some evidence in his room," I said after a while, "a picture or a letter, proof he really is my dad."

Angie stared at me. "Are you thinking what I think you're thinking?"

"He sleeps late, but he's usually gone all afternoon. I could get the spare key easily." We looked at each other, remembering the other times we'd poked and pried through the roomers' belongings. We'd found some odd things — love letters to Miss Lucas from Mr. Walker, a dirty-joke book under Mr. Schumann's socks, and a bottle of hair restorer in Mr. Plummer's room. Clint's room, though, would be the biggest challenge and certainly the most interesting.

"Do you want to do it tomorrow?" Angie pulled a strand of gum out of her mouth and wrapped it around her finger.

"Come over and we'll get the key the minute he leaves," I urged.

"What about your grandmother?" Angie stuffed her gum back in her mouth and chomped on it like a nervous horse. I knew she was thinking of the day Grandmother had found us in Miss Lucas's room, experimenting with her makeup. She had put on her best teacher act and scared us both half to death, especially Angie. It's bad enough to get in trouble with a teacher at school. It's even worse, though, at home.

"She won't catch us, I promise."

"Your grandmother's no dummy," Angie muttered.

"Well, neither am I."

Unfortunately, Angie looked a little skeptical, but she didn't say anything.

Hearing Grandmother calling me, I stood up. "I'll see you tomorrow. Right?"

"Right," I heard Angie mumble as I ran around her house toward home.

CHAPTER · 11

The next day, Angie and I hung around the house, waiting for Clint to leave. By the time he finally came downstairs, we were glassy eyed from watching old TV shows. Lucy, Mister Ed, Beaver, and Dobie Gillis one after the other can practically destroy your brain.

The minute Clint's van chugged off down Main Street, Angie and I slipped into the kitchen and took the key from its hook behind the door. Checking to make sure Grandmother was going to be busy in her garden for a while, we tiptoed upstairs. Miss Lucas's door was shut, but we could hear her radio playing softly. Mr. Schumann was putting in his daily eight hours at the library in Mount Pleasant; he wouldn't be home until four in the afternoon.

As quietly as possible, I turned the key and led Angie into Clint's room. Before I closed the door, Holmes followed us and disappeared under the bed.

"The bureau first," I whispered. Opening the top drawer, I carefully shifted Clint's socks aside, but there was nothing under them. The second and third drawer held T-shirts and underwear, and the bottom drawer was empty.

With growing disappointment, I turned to the washstand beside the bed. When I pulled the drawer open, though, I saw a brown envelope. Inside were two pictures in faded color. In both, Clint was holding a baby. I stared at the tiny face, trying to believe I was looking at myself, but the photograph was really out of focus.

We turned the picture over, but nothing was written on the back, not even a date. And the surroundings were unidentifiable. Clint was leaning against an old car, a Ford or a Dodge, Angie thought. Behind him was a nondescript bungalow, the kind you see in towns everywhere. Sherlock Holmes himself wouldn't have had much luck with the evidence we'd discovered so far.

"How about the wardrobe?" I crossed the room and opened the door. A few shirts, a faded denim jacket, and a navy-blue windbreaker hung on the hangers, but their pockets were empty. On the floor were a pair of well-worn running shoes and an old pair of cowboy boots.

"Aren't these neat?" I picked up the boots to show them to Angie. One of them was very heavy. Putting it down, I stuck my hand inside and pulled out a bulky rag-wool sock. Wrapped in it was a pistol.

"Oh, my God," Angie gasped. "Is it real?"

I nodded. Its weight told me it was not a toy.

"Put it down," she whispered, her eyes wide with fright. "It might be loaded."

With shaking hands, I wrapped the sock around the gun and returned it gently to the boot. Very carefully, I put everything back into the wardrobe and closed the door.

"What does he need a gun for?" Angie whispered.

"I don't know." Shivering a little, I backed away from the wardrobe. The sight and feel of a real gun had scared me.

"Maybe somebody's after him," Angie suggested. "You know, just like you always pretended."

Thinking of the stories I used to make up, I hoped to heaven Clint's enemy wouldn't find him here in Hilltop, not in my grandmother's house, not in the room right next to mine.

"We'd better get out of here," I said. Just knowing there was a gun in the room changed everything.

"But we haven't looked in the desk yet." Angie crossed the room and opened the drawer. Inside was a spiral-bound notebook, the kind you buy for school. She opened it and riffled through the pages.

"Dates and addresses." She frowned and shook her head. "Doesn't make sense."

As she dropped it back into the drawer, I heard the unmistakable sound of Clint's van pulling into the driveway. Without a word, Angie and I headed for the door and opened it. As we pulled it shut behind us, Miss Lucas stepped out into the hall, all dressed up for her afternoon rendezvous with Mr. Walker.

"What are you girls doing?" she asked sharply.

Thinking fast, I said, "Grandmother asked me to put clean towels in Clint's room."

Without waiting for her to ask another question, Angie and I ran downstairs and almost collided with Clint as he opened the front door.

"Hey, what's the rush?" he asked.

"Angie has to go home," I said as we dodged around him.

Without looking back, we dashed across the street and into Angie's house. Safely in her room, with the door shut, we flopped down on her bed, causing a small avalanche of clothes, books, and shoes to slide to the floor.

"Boy, was that close." Angie picked up her old bear Tedward and hugged him tight. "Do you think Miss Lucas will tell on us?"

"I hope not."

I knelt on the bed and looked out the window at our house. Miss Lucas was walking down the sidewalk, clutching her purse as if she expected a mugger to accost her on Main Street. Of Clint there was no sign.

"Maybe he hunts with that gun." Angie held Tedward by his front paws and bounced him up and down, making him do a little dance. "Teddy bear, teddy bear, touch your toes," she crooned, bending poor old Tedward's nose toward his feet.

"Angie, can't you ever keep your mind on anything? People don't hunt with pistols." I snatched

Tedward away from her. "This could be serious. My father could be in some sort of danger."

"If he is your father." Angie frowned and grabbed Tedward back. "You don't know for sure. The baby in that picture could be *anybody*. Even me."

"How could the baby be you?" I stared at Angie. "Your father is coming up the hill right this minute." I pointed out the window at Mr. Wilkins, just getting home from his job at the Sunoco station.

Angie shrugged elaborately. "Just because someone says he's your father doesn't mean he is," she said, flipping her hair. "I could be adopted, you know. Lots of people don't know who their real parents are."

"I'm going home." I paused at the bedroom door. "You sure act dumb sometimes."

"So do you," Angie said without looking at me.

As I left the house, I almost bumped into Mr. Wilkins. "Don't I have enough kids of my own to fall over without adding the neighbors?" he muttered as I squeezed past him.

Poor Angie, I thought as I crossed the street. If Mr. Wilkins were my father, I'd hope I was adopted too.

CHAPTER·12

The sight of Clint sitting on the front porch chased all thoughts of Angie and her father right out of my head. With Holmes in his lap, he was rocking slowly back and forth, watching me walk toward him.

"Hello, Madigan," he said. "I bet you'd never guess what I found in my room today."

I stared at the double reflection of myself in Clint's glasses. Had Angie or I left something behind?

Clint stroked Holmes. "This fellow was curled up in my wardrobe, sound asleep." Scratching Holmes gently behind the ears, he added, "How do you suppose he got there?"

I remembered then that Holmes had followed Angie and me into Clint's room. In our haste to leave, we'd forgotten all about him. "Grandmother must have changed your towels or something," I said weakly. "He probably went in with her, and she didn't notice."

Handing Holmes to me, Clint said, "That could explain it, I suppose."

I took a deep breath, thinking I was safe, and opened the screen door to go inside.

"The only problem is," Clint went on as he followed me into the hall, "your grandmother changes the linen every Wednesday. Today is Thursday."

His voice was low, and the hand he placed on my shoulder held me tightly. "I'd hate to think my favorite girl detectives were spying on me."

For a few seconds, we stood in the hall like a pair of statues, Clint staring down at me, me staring up at him. He'd taken off his sunglasses, and there was no mistaking the anger in his eyes. "I told your grandmother I value my privacy," he said.

"We wouldn't go in your room," I lied. "Not ever!"

"I hope not. I'd like to trust the people I live with."

"You can trust me," I told him, knowing it was true. No matter what he'd done or why he had the gun, I would never betray Clint.

Before he could say anything else, Grandmother stuck her head out of the kitchen and called to me. "Madigan, come give me a hand with dinner."

Clint released me, and I ran to the kitchen. The whole time I was chopping the salad ingredients, I kept thinking about Clint and the gun. I couldn't forget the scary feel of it in my hand, its weight, its smell, its realness.

Glancing at Grandmother standing at the stove, her back to me, I wished I could tell her about it, but I was afraid she'd ask Clint to leave. I'd heard her say more than once that America would never be a civilized country until handguns were outlawed. She didn't believe that anyone had the right to own one, not even the police. "They get along all right without them in England," she always said. "And they have a lot fewer murders than we do."

Making it all the more complicated, of course, were the circumstances. Grandmother would know I'd been snooping in Clint's room if I told her about the gun, and, as Angie had reminded me just yesterday, Grandmother didn't want me going into anyone's room but my own. It was wrong to invade someone else's privacy, she said, and I'd promised never to do it again.

Oddly enough, though, Clint himself brought the subject up at the dinner table. Miss Lucas was talking about the wave of robberies in Mount Pleasant. "You could at least be more careful about locking the house," she told Grandmother. "The front door is open all day, even when no one is home, and for half the night, too."

"I've told you before, Marie, we live in a small town where we know and trust our neighbors," Grandmother replied.

"The Roses were so trusting, they left their keys in the car, and look what happened to them." Miss Lucas stabbed at her salad, her little mouth pursed up tight.

"Arthur Whipple is in jail now, Marie."

"What about his brother Calvin? I see him hanging out in the park with Tom Aitcheson, drinking beer in the middle of the day and smoking God knows what." Miss Lucas leaned toward Grandmother, shaking a forkful of lettuce at her. "If you ask me, those two are responsible for the thefts in Mount Pleasant. They could easily strike here next, but you won't even take the trouble to lock the door."

As Grandmother opened her mouth to defend herself, Clint turned to Miss Lucas. "I think you're absolutely right," he said softly, taking everybody by surprise. "When I lived in the city, I was forced to buy a gun for my own protection. I'm sure I'll never need it here in Hilltop, but I think houses should be locked no matter where you live. Why make it easy for guys like Tom Aitcheson?"

"You have a gun?" Grandmother stared at Clint as if he'd just confessed to committing a horrible crime.

"Yes, I do," Clint said. "Does that bother you, Mrs. Porter?"

Grandmother nodded. "It certainly does. I've never permitted one in this house."

"It's not loaded," Clint said, glancing at me, "and I keep it well hidden."

Miss Lucas stared at Clint, her fork still poised, her lettuce untouched. "Guns terrify me," she said in a high, breathless voice.

"I find them fascinating myself," Mr. Schumann said. "What kind is it?"

Ignoring Mr. Schumann, Grandmother said to

Clint, "You'll have to get rid of it or find somewhere else to stay." Her voice was firm and hard, and I knew she was absolutely serious.

A little silence fell, and I stared at Grandmother, horrified. I wanted to argue, to tell her she was over-reacting, but she was wearing her teacher face, and I knew it was useless.

"I'll take it into Fredericktown tomorrow," Clint said. "I'm sure I can find a gun shop there." Pushing his chair back, he stood up. "I'm sorry I upset you, Mrs. Porter," he said as he left the room.

Before anyone could stop me, I ran outside after Clint. I caught up with him as he was about to get in his van. Grabbing his arm, I stared up at his face. "I would never have told," I cried, "never in a million years!"

Gently, he pulled away from me. "So you did go in my room."

I nodded, crying now. "I'm sorry, I know I shouldn't have."

He sighed and gave my braid a little tug. "Kids and cats," he said.

"What do you mean?"

"They're both too curious."

"Are you mad?"

"Well, frankly, I'm a little disappointed in you, Madigan." He tilted his head to the side, tipping my reflection in his glasses. "What were you looking for, anyway?"

I wanted to tell him the truth, but I just couldn't. It didn't seem the right time to ask if he was my father.

So I said instead, "Angie and I always used to look at Mr. Plummer's stuff. He had all these old pictures in a shoe box in the wardrobe, and we thought they might still be there."

I couldn't see Clint's eyes, but I was pretty sure he didn't believe me. "How would you like it if I snooped through your belongings?" he asked.

I shrugged and wiped my eyes with the back of my hand. "You can look at anything you like," I told him. "You can even read my diary. I wouldn't keep anything secret from you."

He laughed and got into his van. "You're a sweet kid," he said. "But don't ever let anybody know all your secrets, Madigan."

Then he threw the van into gear and drove off, leaving me standing there with Holmes twining around my legs, purring for his dinner.

CHAPTER · 13

A couple of days later, Angie and I were sitting on my front porch steps trying to think of something to do. We'd stopped speaking for a couple of days as a result of our last quarrel, but Angie had finally apologized, probably because she was tired of watching television and fighting with her brothers.

Clint had gotten up early to go fishing. I was disappointed that he hadn't invited me, but, as Angie reminded me, fathers are like that.

"The only place my dad ever takes me is to church," she said. "And the only reason he does that is because Mom makes him. I'm sure he'd rather stay home and read the paper."

Angie bent over and picked at the nail polish on her toes. "It's coming off already. Cheap stuff."

"Good morning, girls." Mr. Schumann eased himself down onto the step next to me and opened his paper. "Look at this," he pointed to the headline. " 'Crime Wave in Frederick County Hits Locust Hill,' " he read. "Three houses were broken into last night, and the police have no suspects. This is really going to send poor Marie up the walls."

"Just Locust Hill?" Angie asked fearfully. "Not anywhere else in town?"

"Don't worry, Angie. This guy is after the big stuff," Mr. Schumann said. "The police think he's the same one who's been robbing houses in Mount Pleasant and Fredericktown. Apparently he's a real professional — knows how to get into the houses, find the valuables, and get out without leaving fingerprints behind. So far, no one has seen him."

I scratched a mosquito bite on my arm until a drop of blood welled up. "Do they think he's dangerous?"

Mr. Schumann paused to light his pipe. "Nobody's confronted him yet, Madigan," he said as he puffed to keep it going. "Who knows what a criminal will do if he's cornered? He may be armed, he may not be. He may shoot, he may not."

In spite of the warm August sun, I shivered a little, remembering Clint's gun. It was the only real gun I'd ever seen, and I hoped he'd gotten rid of it. Having a weapon like that in the house was just too scary.

"What's the matter, Madigan?" Mr. Schumann smiled at me. "Surely you're not afraid of a burglar."

I laughed and flipped my braid over my shoulder, and Holmes immediately pounced on it as if he had been lying in ambush just to catch my hair.

"Madigan's not scared of anything," Angie said

loyally. "And neither am I. If that thief ever meets us, he'll be sorry."

"Do you think it's Tom Aitcheson?" I asked Mr. Schumann. "Or Calvin Whipple?"

Mr. Schumann chuckled. "No matter what Marie thinks, those guys are too dumb to pull off anything like this. Look at Arthur. He didn't even get a mile out of town before he wrecked the Rose's car."

"Then who?"

Mr. Schumann shook his head. "Somebody from Fredericktown, maybe. Or even Baltimore. As Marie says, we're not that far from the big city anymore."

Mr. Schumann turned his attention to other news in the paper, and I gazed across the lawn at the mountains, contemplating what he had said about the robber. Like Miss Lucas, I myself had suspected Tom Aitcheson and Calvin Whipple. They were certainly the only real criminals in Hilltop. Neither one of them had a job, and they were always getting arrested for breaking windows and setting off firecrackers and spray painting graffiti on the elementary school wall.

But Mr. Schumann was right — they were dumb. Like Arthur, they always got caught.

Restlessly I turned to Angie. "Let's walk down to Sweeney's and get a Coke," I suggested.

"I don't have any money," Angie said.

"You never do." I stood up. "Come on, I'll treat."

We waved good-bye to Mr. Schumann, who told us to watch out for suspicious strangers, and strolled down the hill to Sweeney's. Unfortunately Richard was too busy to give us free refills, so we browsed around the drugstore for a while, spraying ourselves with sample perfumes and leafing through magazines until Mr. Sweeney suggested that we leave.

Out in the sun again, we ducked into the hardware store to hide from Kevin and Sean as they rumbled past on their Big Wheels. By a stack of lawn fertilizer bags, we saw Mr. Walker and Miss Lucas whispering about something, but when we tried to sneak close enough to hear their conversation, Julie Piranesi spotted us.

"Did you know our house was robbed while we were in Ocean City?" she asked importantly.

We shook our heads, and she told us all the details, right down to the last antique doll. "That's why I'm in here. My father's getting a burglar alarm." She pointed at Doctor Piranesi, who was examining a display of electronic equipment.

"Everybody in Locust Hill is scared to death," Julie went on. "Three houses have been robbed — ours, the Griffins', and the Feldmans'." Her small eyes widened and her plump cheeks quivered. "Is your grandmother getting an alarm?"

"We haven't got anything a thief would want," I said.

"He takes antiques," Julie said. "And my mother said your grandmother's old silver is worth a fortune. You better tell her to get some security."

I shrugged. "My grandmother has more important things to worry about."

I tried to sound totally unconcerned, but as Angie and I left the store, I wondered if Grandmother was being a little careless. Even Clint had agreed with Miss Lucas about the importance of locking up. Maybe I'd start double-checking the doors before I went to bed, just to be sure they were locked.

I was thinking so hard, Angie saw Clint before I did. "Look who's going into Greene's," she whispered, digging her nails into my arm.

I looked across the street just in time to see him disappear through the door.

"I thought he was fishing," Angie said.

"Me too." Without a word, we dashed across the street and peered through a display of pots and pans in the window.

"There he is," I said, "talking to Alice."

"Let's sneak up on them and hear what they're saying," Angie whispered.

We waited for Mrs. Appleton to open the door and then we followed her into the store. Crouching down to avoid being seen, we scuttled along the aisle parallel to notions, hoping no one would ask us what we were doing. When we were opposite Clint and Alice, we raised our heads cautiously and saw them talking in voices too low to hear. Alice looked upset, and all of a sudden she said more loudly, "I told you I can't, I just can't."

"Oh, come on," Clint said. He was standing with his back to us, his weight on one hip, his hands in his pockets. I wished I could see his face.

"I said no." Alice bent her head, and her hair slid down over her eyes. "Now get out of here before you make me lose my job."

Clint shrugged and mumbled something I couldn't hear. Then he walked off, brushing past Mrs. Appleton, who was examining a display of necklaces. Alice watched him leave, and for a minute I thought she was going to call him back. But Mrs. Piranesi handed her a bunch of stuff and Alice had to wait on her instead.

"Come on," I whispered to Angie, "let's see where he's going."

By the time we hit the sidewalk, Clint was a block away and strolling toward his van. Ducking along from tree to tree, we kept him in sight till he drove away.

"Darn," Angie muttered. "I wish we had a car."

"We'll go back and see Alice," I said. "Maybe she'll tell us what's going on."

CHAPTER · 14

When Angie and I walked into Greene's, we saw Alice straightening up the necklace display. Mrs. Appleton had moved on to the lingerie counter, leaving Alice to restore some order to the strings of plastic beads.

Leaning casually against the counter, I said, "I didn't know you knew Clint James."

Alice glanced at me. "That guy who's renting a room at your house?"

I nodded, wanting to add yes, that guy who just happens to be my father. But I only looked at her, thinking she wasn't as pretty as she used to be. "I saw him in here a few minutes ago."

"What's it to you, Madigan?" Alice pushed her hair out of her eyes and frowned at me. "Is there a law against talking to your grandmother's roomers?"

"Did he ask you out or something?" Angie wanted to know.

For an answer, Alice snatched the necklace Angie was trying to fasten around her neck. "Keep your grubby little hands off the merchandise," she said crossly.

"What did he say to put you in such a bad mood?" Angie asked.

"He didn't say *anything*," Alice said. "He just wanted to buy something."

"You don't usually get all upset with customers," I put in, "the way you were with Clint."

"You know something, Madigan?" Alice gave me a long look. "You're too nosy for your own good."

"I bet you think he's handsome, though, don't you?" Angie nudged me and giggled. "You probably wouldn't mind going dancing with him sometime." She tried to make me do a twirl with her, but I pulled away and bumped into Mrs. Appleton, who was riffling through a display of handkerchiefs behind me.

"Can I help you?" Alice leaned toward Mrs. Appleton, but the old lady shook her head.

"Oh, goodness me, no," she said. "You just go right on with your conversation, my dear. Don't let me interrupt you."

Smiling and nodding, Mrs. Appleton backed away, making me suspect she'd been filling her canvas bag with goodies from Alice's counter. But I had too much else on my mind to care.

"Listen," Alice said when the old lady was gone. "I need you all to babysit again." She bent her head to examine her fingernails, and her hair slid down across her face, hiding her eyes.

"You're going dancing with Clint, right?" Angie winked at me.

Ignoring Angie, Alice went on. "You have to pick Chad up at Brenda Pfeiffer's house at seven o'clock. You know where she lives, don't you?"

"Why do we have to walk all the way over there?" Angie asked.

"She's my daytime babysitter, and she can't keep Chad later than seven tonight." Alice started straightening the pile of handkerchiefs Mrs. Appleton had left behind. "I can pay you each five dollars like before," she said.

"What do we do after we get Chad?" I asked.

"Take him to the park. They're having outdoor movies starting at dusk. Tom and Jerry and Porky Pig and Donald Duck. I'll meet you there around ten."

"Okay," Angie said. "But you better not be late. I don't want to hang around any old park after dark, not with some thief robbing houses all over the place."

"Thanks," Alice said. "Be sure to get to Brenda's on time. She's got a date tonight, and I promised her you'd be there to pick up Chad."

Outside in the hot sun, I turned to Angie. "I sure would like to know who Alice is going out with."

"It's Clint, I bet anything," Angie said.

I shook my head so hard my braid swung out and thunked Angie. "You heard what she said. She doesn't like him. Anybody could tell that from the way she was acting."

Angie shrugged. "Maybe she met somebody at the

Lone Star Tavern. A married man, like in those songs they always play on 'Country Swing.' Alice meets him on the wrong side of town so his wife won't find out."

"I hope not," I said. "Alice should marry somebody who'd take her away from here. Her and Chad both." Far away, I thought to myself, and the sooner the better. The scene between her and Clint kept flashing in front of my eyes like an instant replay on TV, and it made me uneasy. Suppose he fell in love with Alice and I had to share him with her?

Angie stuck a fresh piece of gum in her mouth. "Who's she going to meet in Hilltop? Everybody with any sense leaves here as soon as he can." She blew a bubble and started across the street toward her house. "See you at quarter of seven," she called.

"It's about time you two got here." Brenda was sitting on the sagging porch of a little bungalow watching Angie and me walk up the sidewalk. Chad was playing in the dirt nearby, and Tom Aitcheson was lounging in the doorway, wearing his usual outfit — a denim jacket with the sleeves ripped out and faded jeans.

"How's your sister?" Tom asked Angie as she strapped Chad into his stroller. "I haven't seen much of her lately."

Angie kept her head bent as she fastened the buckle. "She's fine."

"I told you Alice has been busy lately." Brenda frowned at Tom and tossed her hair. If there's one person in Hilltop Miss Lucas dislikes more than Alice, it's Brenda. I heard her tell Grandmother once that Brenda was the town tramp, though, as far as I know, Brenda has never set foot outside Hilltop in her entire life.

"You're turning into a real looker, you know that?" Tom grinned at Angie. "In a few years, you'll be driving all the guys crazy. Maybe I'll give you a call when you're about sixteen."

Hearing this, Brenda gave Tom a mean look. "Are we going out or not?"

"Sure, babe." Tom tossed his cigarette into the bushes and winked at Angie. Then he straddled his motorcycle and Brenda climbed on behind him. Neither one of them bothered to put on a helmet. They just roared off into the evening, leaving Angie and me to push Chad down the road to the playground.

"What a jerk," I said. "No matter who Alice is dating, he's got to be better than Tom."

Angie nodded, but then she looked at me, her face serious. "Do you think I really will be pretty?"

I looked at her and sighed. "You already are pretty. You don't need some guy like Tom to tell you, either."

Angie smiled, obviously pleased. "Prettier than Alice?" she asked.

"Much prettier," I said, "and smarter too. You won't go off and get pregnant and end up working for Greene's. You and me — we'll go to college and then we'll set up our detective agency in some exciting place — San Francisco or New Orleans, maybe even London or Paris." The names of these cities felt good in my mouth, and, as I spoke, I could see Angie and me walking along the Seine, not far from the Eiffel Tower, the sky turning pink just as it was here in Hilltop and all the lights of Paris sparkling.

But Angie just sighed. "I don't know if I want to be a detective anymore," she said softly. "I kind of think I might want to work as an airline hostess for a while. You can see the world that way too, Madigan. Then I might just get married and have lots of cute little babies like Chad."

As she bent over the stroller laughing down at Chad, I glanced at Angie, and it shocked me to realize she was growing up faster than I was. How come I hadn't noticed those bumps under her T-shirt? Pretty soon she was going to have a real figure, but I was as little and scrawny as ever. And I was seven-and-a-half months older than she was.

Instead of getting mad at her for wanting to be an airline hostess, I plodded along beside her feeling depressed. When we started junior high in the fall, she was going to be really popular, I thought. And me? I'd be lucky if she stayed my best friend.

Then I remembered Clint. Maybe when he revealed the truth to me about our relationship, he'd take me away from Hilltop. Back to California or something, and we'd be together, just the two of us, and he'd be my best friend. Then it wouldn't matter what Angie did — I'd be far away, and Clint and I could be a father-and-daughter detective team.

CHAPTER · 15

By the time we got to the park, the sun had dropped behind the mountains and the blues and pinks of the sky were graying into darkness. The screen, a white sheet, was stretched between two poles cemented into tires. In front of it, parents were spreading blankets and setting up little folding lawn chairs while their kids ran around yelling and screaming. Naturally Angie and I hadn't thought to bring anything to sit on.

"Wing, wing!" Chad scrambled out of his stroller and ran toward the swings on his short legs. We chased after him, laughing because he looked like a little windup doll.

After we'd taken turns pushing him for about fifteen minutes, the first cartoon started, a Tom and Jerry. "Come on, Chaddy." I lifted him out of the swing. "Let's go watch the smart little mice and the big dumb cat."

As usual the mice ran circles around Tom, trapping him in the refrigerator, practically killing him by turning the kitchen floor into an ice-skating rink, bombarding him with cans of food. I laughed till my sides hurt, glad to get my mind off the changes I saw in Angie. And she laughed too, just like always.

After three cartoons, Chad started getting restless. For one thing, it was dark. All around us kids were eating popcorn and watermelon and drinking Kool-Aid from big thermos jugs while they lounged on blankets and quilts. Here we were, sitting on the damp grass with nothing to eat or drink and no money to buy anything. It was no wonder Chad began fussing.

"Where Mommy?" he asked Angie.

"She'll be here soon, Chaddy." Angie was holding him on her lap, but he squirmed away.

"Want Mommy, want juicey!" Chad cried.

"Hey, shut that kid up!" somebody yelled. The Road Runner was zooming along in his little dust cloud, and Coyote was about to get blown up by the dynamite he didn't know was attached to his tail instead of his enemy's.

"How about a nice ride in a swing?" I picked Chad up, and Angie and I started inching our way through the crowd, trying not to step on anybody's blanket. I could just see myself putting my foot right in the middle of a bowl of potato salad or something.

"Get down in front!" somebody else yelled. It sounded like Kevin, so I hurried and managed to kick over a can of soda, which nobody noticed at the moment.

When I tried to put Chad in the swing, he stiffened his body and cried, "No, no! Want Mommy!"

"Mommy's coming," I told him. "Don't you want to sit in the nice swing?"

"No! No!"

As Chad continued to wail and squirm, I heard a familiar cry. I turned to Angie, but it was too late to hide.

"It's Badagain Baloney and Angie!" Kevin yelled as he and Sean ran toward us.

"Is Mom with you?" Angie asked.

"She's back there somewhere with Mrs. O'Hara and Mrs. Rose." Kevin jerked his thumb back toward the crowd watching Coyote explode. "Is that *Chad?*"

Angie gulped and shook her head hard. "Of course not!"

"He sure looks like him." Kevin bent down and stared hard at Chad. "What's your name?"

Chad started to cry and hid his face behind Angie's leg. "Mommy," he sobbed, "Mommy."

"His name's Mommy?" Sean looked puzzled.

"You are soooo dumb, Sean," Kevin muttered.

"So are you, you're a dumb stupid-head," Sean said.

"Oh, shut up." Kevin raised his fist menacingly, and Sean cringed. "I'm telling Mom you're babysitting Chad," Kevin said to Angie.

"This is Paul Grant," I told Kevin. "All little kids look alike, dope."

"I'm getting Mom. She'll know."

Angie and I watched Kevin run back toward the audience, followed by Sean who was wailing, "Wait, wait up, you dopey dumbo!"

"Let's get out of here," I said.

Dumping Chad into the stroller, we ran down a dark path toward the lake. There were a lot of bushes, and we figured Mrs. Wilkins wouldn't see us if we could keep Chad from crying. The cool night air rushing into his face seemed to have shocked him into silence at least temporarily.

With our hearts thumping, we crouched down behind a clump of rhododendrons and listened for Kevin's shrill voice. Sometimes he reminds me of kids you see in horror movies like *The Children of the Corn*. I'm sure he'd just love leading a gang of vampires or body snatchers to their victims.

"Mommy, Mommy," Chad whimpered.

"Shush, shush, Chaddy." I picked him up and cuddled him, rocking him in my arms and playing a little tickle-bird game with him.

"What do we do now?" Angie whispered. "How is Alice going to find us?"

I glanced at the luminous dial of my wristwatch. "It's after nine thirty. She should be here soon."

"Shh!" Angie grabbed my arm. "Somebody's coming!"

"Oh, Homer, you are the most romantic man," we heard Miss Lucas say. Peering through the leaves, we saw her walking toward us with Mr. Walker. They were holding hands like teenagers, and Miss Lucas was actually giggling.

"Oh, Marie, my Marie," Mr. Walker sang. Then they stopped and put their arms around each other. They kissed for so long I wondered how they breathed.

"I hear something." Miss Lucas pulled away from Mr. Walker and smoothed her hair. "Let's go, Homer."

"How about coming back to my place?" Mr. Walker whispered as he passed us, but all Miss Lucas did was giggle.

"Look, it's Alice." I nudged Angie, who was still choking with laughter. "And she's with someone."

In the darkness, we could see Alice's hair glimmering in the moonlight, but a tree blocked us from seeing who she was with. Her voice carried back to us, though. "I still think it's a bad idea," she was saying. "Besides, he's too little to understand."

The other voice was so low, we couldn't hear a word it said. The locusts chirped, the crickets peeped, and on the lake a bullfrog croaked, all interfering with our hearing.

"Maybe it would be better if you just went away," Alice said, but she didn't sound as if she really meant it.

We heard the other voice mumble something, and Alice stepped out of sight behind the tree. There was a long silence. Chad had apparently dozed off, and

Angie and I were afraid to move. If he woke up, he would surely cry again and give us away.

When Alice finally reappeared, my legs felt numb from squatting so long in the damp grass.

"You know I still love you, I can't help it." Alice backed toward us. "But I have to think about Chad, what's best for him."

A hand reached out and closed around her arm, drawing her gently out of sight again. This time she stayed behind the tree even longer than before, and I would have given anything to creep closer and see what she was doing.

"I have to go." Alice smoothed her dress and hair. "You leave now, okay? And tomorrow I'll bring him."

Without looking back, Alice ran right past us and disappeared around a curve in the path. Signaling me to stay still, Angie crept toward the tree. She made more noise than I would have, and when she came back she had nothing to report.

"Nobody was there," she said. "Not a sign of him. I don't know how he disappeared so fast."

Disappointed, I heaved myself stiffly to my feet, waking Chad in the process. He began to cry, so I carried him while Angie pushed the stroller.

"I hope Alice doesn't run into Mom," Angie said. "I'll really get in trouble if she finds out I was babysitting Chad."

When we got back to the playground, the cartoons were over and the crowd had disappeared. Alice was standing by the swings, looking for us.

"Where have you been?" she cried when she spotted us. She snatched Chad out of my arms and cuddled him. "Yes, yes, honey, Mommy's here."

"We had to hide," I explained. "Kevin and Sean saw us. We told them he wasn't Chad, but Kevin was going to get your mother. We knew we couldn't fool her."

"Who were you talking to?" Angie asked Alice. "Back there by the lake?"

Alice stared at Angie over Chad's head. "You saw him?" Her voice was high and tight, and she looked scared.

"No, but I heard you telling him all kinds of stuff about Chad. Was it his father?" Angie rocked the empty stroller back and forth and chomped her gum, watching Alice through narrowed eyes.

Alice thrust our babysitting money at us, shoved Chad into his stroller, and started walking briskly up the sidewalk. "Just shut up, Angie," she snarled over her shoulder. "And stay out of my life!"

"You are so weird," Angie called, running along behind her. "I'm never babysitting for you again!"

"Good!" Alice yelled. "I don't plan to ask you!"

As Angie tried to catch up with Alice, I grabbed her arm. "Leave her alone," I said. "Can't you see she's all upset?"

Angie shook my hands off, but she didn't go after her sister. Instead, she stood beside me at the entrance to the park and watched Alice disappear into the alley by the drugstore.

"I still think it's Clint," Angie muttered.

"Well, *I* don't." I glared at Angie, feeling myself getting angry. "Like you said, it's probably some married guy."

"But the argument they were having in Greene's," Angie said. "It was almost the same."

"So?" I twisted my braid around my finger. More than anything, I wanted Angie to shut up. I just didn't feel like thinking about Alice — I was too tired, and I needed to go to bed and sleep and sleep and sleep.

Angie glanced at me. The moonlight washed out the color in her face and hair, making her look as pale as a fish swimming in the deepest part of the ocean. "You know what I think?" she asked me.

I shook my head and started walking the few blocks toward home, but Angie kept on talking anyway. "I think you're jealous of Alice. You want Clint all to yourself."

"He's my father, isn't he?" I didn't look at her, but my chest felt as if somebody had wrapped wires around it and pulled them tight.

"Maybe he is and maybe he isn't," Angie said. "I think probably he isn't. You're just making up fairy tales about him like you did when we were little."

By this time we were at the top of the hill, and I was practically running away from Angie. "Why don't you shut up?" I yelled at her.

"Why don't you?" she shouted back.

"Angie?" Mrs. Wilkins's voice rose above my retort. "Get in here right this minute! I want to talk to you, young lady!"

For a second Angie and I looked at each other,

forgetting to be mad. "Kevin told," Angie muttered, "and Mom's going to kill me. It's a good thing those dumb guns of his aren't real. If they were, I swear I'd shoot him."

As Angie's screen door slammed shut behind her, I walked slowly up the sidewalk toward home. The moonlight made sharp shadows, straight-edged and true on the silvery grass, and a light shone in our living room window where Grandmother sat reading in her favorite chair. The rest of the house was dark, and I knew no light shone from Clint's window. Like Holmes, he was out somewhere, enjoying the night.

Hesitating with my hand on the gate, I made up my mind. I was going to ask Clint to tell me the truth about himself for once and for all. Was he my father? Or wasn't he? I couldn't go on wondering about him, waiting, hoping. I had to know.

CHAPTER · 16

The next day, when I went over to Angie's, Mrs. Wilkins met me at the door with her arms folded firmly across her chest.

"You can forget about seeing Angie today," she said. "She's grounded for a week. Your grandmother may not care who you babysit for, but Angie has strict rules. The sooner she learns to obey them, the better off she'll be."

When Mrs. Wilkins is in a bad mood, she scares me to death, so I ran back home, gathered Holmes into my lap, and sat down on the porch steps. Without Angie, what was I going to do for the next seven days?

"You look gloomy, Madigan." Clint dropped into the rocker next to me. He had the morning paper in one hand and a cup of coffee in the other.

As he made himself comfortable, my heart sped up. Now was my chance to ask him the big question, but the words wouldn't come, not yet. Instead I said, "Angie's in trouble with her mom, and she can't leave her yard for a whole week."

"What did she do?" The sweet smell of coffee rose from his mug and mingled with the scent of Grandmother's flowers. I breathed it in deeply, enjoying being with Clint on such a pretty summer morning.

"Mrs. Wilkins found out we were babysitting Chad last night," I told him. "You know how she feels about Alice."

I watched him sip his coffee, wishing I had the nerve to come right out and ask him how *he* felt about Alice, but something in me held back. Maybe I didn't really want to know. Instead, I asked him where he'd been last night. "You weren't at the park were you, walking by the lake?"

I held my breath, scared to look at him as I waited for him to answer.

"What makes you ask that?" Clint's voice was soft, but it sort of thrummed with something hidden beneath the surface.

"Well, there was a cartoon festival," I said, but I felt so uncomfortable I wished I hadn't asked him anything at all. I was messing up the morning with my nosiness, but I couldn't stop myself. "I thought maybe you liked Tom and Jerry."

Clint didn't say anything. He just rocked slowly back and forth and sipped his coffee.

"Alice was there," I blurted out. "I think Chad's father has come back." This was it, I thought — mentioning Chad's father would be a good way to lead into asking the question that was burning my throat.

Clint stared at me with eyes as blue as the clearest October sky. "What gives you that idea?"

"Angie and I heard Alice talking to somebody at the lake last night," I said uneasily, wishing he'd look at something else with those eyes of his. "From what they were saying, he wants her and Chad to go away with him, but she's not sure she should." My voice trailed off, and I bent my head over Holmes, giving him a lot of attention so I wouldn't have to meet Clint's eyes.

"Did you see the man?" Clint asked.

I shook my head. "He was behind a tree."

Clint took another swallow of coffee and propped his feet on the railing. "What do you think Alice should do, Madigan?"

I stole a glance at him, but he wasn't looking at me anymore. Instead, he was gazing across the yard, past the Wilkinses' house, at the mountains and maybe beyond them at places I'd never seen or even imagined.

"She should go," I whispered. "If my father came for me, I'd go wherever he wanted to take me."

"Even if you had to leave your grandmother?" Clint turned his eyes back to me, and a little shiver ran all over my skin.

I nodded, not even feeling guilty. "Fathers should come first, shouldn't they?"

"I think so," Clint said. For a minute his hand

rested lightly on my head. "You're a good girl, Madigan."

Tears filled my eyes, and I thought, now, now is the time to ask him. But when I opened my mouth, the words were locked up somewhere and they wouldn't come out.

Clint sighed and opened the paper. "Another robbery in Locust Hill," he said. "Aren't you and Angie investigating this case, Madigan?"

"Miss Lucas thinks it's Tom Aitcheson and Calvin Whipple, but they're too dumb to get away without getting caught." I watched a butterfly flutter around the roses, relieved that Clint had changed the subject. Maybe I wasn't quite ready to ask him after all.

"I bet it's Mrs. Appleton," Clint said in a low voice.

He sounded so earnest that I thought for a minute he was serious. "You're kidding."

"Burglary is not a joking matter, Madigan," he said, imitating Miss Lucas perfectly, right down to the little sniff and the upward thrust of her chin.

"No, I mean it," he went on after I'd stopped laughing. "She's so little and light on her feet, I bet she could sneak in and out a window as quietly as Holmes. And who would ever suspect her?"

I laughed again and shook my head. "That's silly."

Clint shrugged and glanced at Holmes. "Maybe it's you," he whispered, scatching Holmes under his chin. "The cat burglar himself."

"Or maybe it's you," I said, laughing. "The mystery man in the silver glasses."

Clint looked startled for a moment, but then he laughed too and spread his hands. "Do I look like a thief?"

I shook my head, still laughing. "Do I?"

Clint stood up and stretched. "You better confess, kid. You're still young enough to reform."

Before I could ask him anything else, he was walking down the steps, heading for his van.

In the silence he left behind, I hugged Holmes till he squirmed. Without Clint to make me laugh, I felt very lonely. Inside the house, I heard Grandmother running the vacuum cleaner, a sure sign she was too busy to talk to me. Mr. Schumann had already gone to Mount Pleasant, and Miss Lucas was sitting in a lawn chair, reading a novel in the shade.

Not wanting her to pounce on me, I walked down Main Street with Holmes trotting beside me. I strolled by Sweeney's and the hardware store and then crossed the street. As I passed the cemetery's wrought iron gate, I stopped and looked inside. Dappled with shade, the mowed grass looked cool and green and peaceful, silent and deserted as usual.

Even though Hilltop is a small town, it's very old, so there are more dead people buried in Ivy Hill Cemetery than there are live people walking around the streets. The graves stretch from Main Street way back to Bender's Alley on the very edge of town. Believe it or not, it's one of my favorite places, cooler than the park and a lot less crowded.

So when Holmes slipped through the gate, his eyes

on a mockingbird pecking in the gravel roadway, I followed him and threaded my way through the angels, crosses, and tombstones to my mother's grave.

Because there have been Porters in Hilltop since the town began, my mother is buried in a family plot in the oldest part of the cemetery, far from the noise of Main Street. When I was little, I used to visit her on the way home from school. Sitting on the grass, I would tell her everything that had happened to me that day. I thought she could hear me, that she would want to know how my life was going.

For the past couple of years, though, I hadn't visited her as often as I used to. And when I did come, I simply put flowers on her grave and tried to remember what she looked like, how her voice sounded, what it was like to sit on her lap and feel her arms around me. Gradually she was slipping away from me, becoming fainter and fainter like a little figure at the end of a long, dark tunnel.

Today I sat down and traced the inscription carved in pink stone: "Megan Elizabeth Maloney, Beloved Daughter of Howard and Florence Porter, June 19, 1953 — November 25, 1978." Next to her lay Howard Porter, my grandfather, who had died in an automobile accident before I was born. They were surrounded by other Porters, young and old, my ancestors. If they could all come back to life, what a big family I'd have.

"What would you think, Mom," I whispered, "if my dad came back. Would you forgive him?"

A soft summer breeze ruffled the leaves on the box-wood growing tall around me, and a mourning dove cooed in the yew trees behind me.

"I wish you could answer," I sighed. "Since I don't have you, I really need my dad."

Feeling truly like a poor motherless child, I lay on my back and gazed up at the big white clouds drifting by. When I was little, I thought Mom watched me from the sky. What if she were looking down now? Would she be happy that my father had come back? She'd been dead so long. Surely she'd forgiven Clint, especially up there in heaven with all those angels singing and playing harps.

The mourning dove called again, even more plaintively. I closed my eyes and let the peaceful sound lull me into a dream of Clint and me and Grandmother living happily together.

I don't know how long I'd been asleep when I was awakened by the sound of a voice on the other side of the boxwood hedge.

"Oh, it's beautiful," I heard Alice say. "Just beautiful."

Startled, I sat up and peered through the thick leaves. To my amazement, I saw Clint fastening a necklace around Alice's neck. Then she threw her arms around him and kissed him while Chad dozed near them in his stroller. As I watched, too shocked to speak, Alice drew back and smiled up at Clint. "And you picked such a good place to hide everything."

"Stick with me, Alice, I'm a clever guy," Clint said, drawing her close and kissing her again.

I crouched beside my mother's grave, trembling with rage. Every good thought I'd ever had about Alice was drowned in a wave of black hatred. How could she sneak around behind my back with my father?

Just then Chad woke up and started fussing. Alice lifted him out of his stroller and handed him to Clint. "Here's your daddy, sweetie," she crooned. "Tell him you want some nice cold juicey."

It was too much. As Clint cuddled Chad, I charged out of the bushes.

"Put him down," I yelled, grabbing at Chad. "You're not his father!"

"Madigan, what the hell are you doing?" Clint stepped backward as Alice yanked me away from Chad.

"Are you crazy?" she screamed at me.

"He's not Chad's father, he can't be!" I cried, trying to break away from Alice.

"What do you mean?" Alice kept a grip on my wrists, preventing me from lunging at Clint again.

"Let go of me!" I kicked at Alice but she side-stepped my bare foot and glared at me, her face red.

"I'll slap your face, you little brat!" Alice said, but before she could hit me, Clint put Chad in his stroller and pulled me roughly away from Alice.

"I'll take care of this," he said to her, "and you see to Chad."

I was crying now, great, gulping sobs, the kind that

won't stop. "You're not his father," I wept, "you're my father!"

Clint stared at me and shook his head. "Oh, Madigan," he said. "Madigan, whatever gave you that idea?"

"That's why you're here, that's why you're staying at my grandmother's house," I sobbed, "to check up on me, to make sure I'm all right. Please tell me the truth, I won't tell Grandmother, I promise I won't."

Clint sighed. "I'm not your father, Madigan. I swear I'm not."

"This is the craziest thing I ever heard," Alice said. She was clutching Chad and glaring at me. The sunlight twinkled on the necklace she wore over her T-shirt, and her face was flushed. "Clint never saw your mother in his life."

I looked at Clint, and he shook his head again. "There's been some kind of misunderstanding, Madigan," he said softly. "Like Alice says, I never met your mother, honey."

With a sudden surge of strength, I pulled away from Clint and ran down the path, away from him and Alice and Chad, away from their calls to come back. A mistake. I'd made a stupid mistake. It wasn't me he'd come to see, but Chad. Chad and Alice!

CHAPTER · 17

When I got home, I ran straight up to my room and cried for a long time. I never wanted to see Clint again, never, never, never. He had fooled me on purpose, I was sure of it, just to tease me. And I hated him for it.

Just this morning, he'd tricked me into saying Alice should go away with him. He'd made me think he was talking about him and me. How could I have been so dumb?

And Alice — I remembered telling Clint she was too good for Tom Aitcheson. I'd even said I wished somebody nice would come along and take her away from Hilltop. Well, it looked like that was exactly what was going to happen!

Worst of all, though, was Angie — she'd never really believed Clint was my father. Wouldn't she gloat when Alice ran off with Clint? I could just hear her going on and on about it, chomping her dumb old gum and claiming she knew it all along. She'd probably say it was the most romantic thing she ever heard and not even care that my heart was broken.

It was stifling hot in my room, but I stayed there all afternoon, crying and tossing around, beating my pillow and carrying on. I felt so bad and stupid I was afraid I was having a nervous breakdown or developing cancer like my mother. All because of Clint, I was either going to lose my mind or die young.

I fell asleep imagining my own funeral. Clint would be there — just him, not Alice — and he would cry and be sorry, but it would be too late. I, Jennifer Madigan Maloney, would be dead and gone, another victim of a broken heart. Grandmother would turn to him and say, "You might as well have put a gun to the poor child's head and pulled the trigger."

I woke up early in the evening, hot and grumpy, with a horrible taste in my mouth. Grandmother was bending over me telling me it was time for dinner.

"I'm not hungry," I moaned, trying to brush my sweaty hair off my face. "I'm sick."

Grandmother laid her hand on my forehead, her way of telling my temperature. "There's not a thing on earth wrong with you," she said, "except you've been sleeping in here on a hot day."

"I feel awful," I whined, but she got me up and led me to the bathroom.

"Wash your face and brush your teeth," she said firmly. "Then come down to dinner."

Well, the last thing in the world I wanted was to sit at a table with Clint, but there was no arguing with Grandmother. Without looking at Clint, I slid into my chair and picked at my food, feeding most of it to Holmes when nobody was looking.

Before long, Miss Lucas brought up her favorite topic. "I wish they'd catch that thief," she said. "It scares me to death just thinking about him. Last night I was sure I heard footsteps on the stairs."

"It was probably me," Clint said. "I came in late."

"You always come in late," Miss Lucas said coldly.

As I bent my head over my plate, I glanced at Clint. He was staring at the little rainbow shadows Miss Lucas's rings cast on the white tablecloth. I'd seen the same watchful interest in Holmes's eyes when he crouched on the porch railing watching a robin hop across the lawn.

After dinner, Clint caught my arm. "I want to talk to you," he said softly, but I pulled away from him.

"Well, I don't want to talk to you!" I glared at him. "Not ever again."

"Madigan," he said, stretching his hand toward me.

"Go talk to Alice," I whispered, "or Chad. Just leave me alone."

Without looking back at him, I left him standing in the hall and fled to the safety of the kitchen and Grandmother. To her surprise, I threw my arms around her and hugged her tight. "I love you," I said fiercely, "I love you."

"Why, I love you too, Madigan." She kissed the

top of my head and handed me a dish towel. "How about giving me a hand?"

While Grandmother and I washed the dishes, she said, "You were awfully quiet at dinner tonight, Madigan."

"I told you I didn't feel good," I mumbled.

"Maybe you should go to bed early, then," she said. Drying her hands, she laid her palm on my forehead again. "Still no sign of a fever."

I hesitated before going upstairs, wishing I could talk to Grandmother. But she had already settled down to watch "Great Performances" on television, and I knew she wouldn't want me interrupting an opera to talk about my father. Slowly I went upstairs and got into bed, even though it was barely dark.

To avoid thinking about Clint, I started reading a new Agatha Christie murder mystery, but my thoughts kept straying back to that horrible scene in the graveyard. Why had Alice been talking about a hiding place? And where had Clint gotten the necklace he had given her?

Suddenly I had an idea — suppose Clint was the thief the police were looking for? As I thought it over, everything fell into place: his late hours, his gun, his secretiveness. Hadn't the houses in Locust Hill been robbed after I'd told him about them? Why, he'd probably stolen the necklace he gave to Alice. Was the rest of the stuff hidden in the graveyard? Was that what Alice meant?

Lying there gazing out the window, I had an irresistible thought — what if I went to Ivy Hill and found the things Clint had stolen? I was pretty sure he'd hidden them somewhere near my mother's grave. All I'd have to do was find them and then go to the police. It wouldn't be dangerous at all.

And I'd be famous. My picture would be in the paper under the headline "Local Girl Solves Mystery." Smiling with satisfaction, I imagined Angie's face when she heard the news. She wouldn't laugh at me then for making a stupid mistake about Clint, not when I was a celebrity.

And Clint wouldn't laugh, either. He'd realize I wasn't a dumb kid daydreaming about being a detective. Because of me, he'd get taken to jail, and it would serve him right.

Best of all, Alice wouldn't go anywhere with Clint. She'd have to stay right here in Hilltop for the rest of her life, and she'd probably end up marrying Tom Aitcheson. Or, better yet, Calvin Whipple, who was even grungier than Tom.

I looked at my clock radio. Not quite ten o'clock — much too early to worry about Clint coming to the graveyard with any more loot. All I had to do was get dressed, grab a flashlight, and sneak out of the house. Then a quick search of Ivy Hill and a visit to the police station. An hour at the most, I thought, and I'd be safely back in bed, and the police would be lying in wait for Clint. It was perfectly safe.

So why did I hesitate? Well, there was the gun, for one thing. I no longer believed Clint had gotten rid of it just because Grandmother told him to. No, I was sure he still had it, hidden in his van or something.

Uneasily I remembered what Mr. Schumann had said about criminals. You could never be sure what they'd do. Maybe they'd shoot you, maybe they wouldn't. But I wasn't going to see Clint, I reminded myself, he wasn't going to be in the graveyard.

When I sat up, Holmes meowed softly, his eyes shining in the darkness. As he stretched and yawned, I stroked his soft fur. Then he slid out from under my hand, leaped to the windowsill, and meowed again, a little louder this time.

"You want to go out, don't you?" I whispered as he rubbed against the screen, purring.

"Okay," I said, "only this time I'll go with you."

Telling myself Holmes would somehow protect me if anything went wrong, I peeled off my pajamas and pulled on a navy-blue T-shirt, a pair of dark jeans, and my running shoes. Then I grabbed a flashlight from my underwear drawer, pushed the screen up silently, and crawled out onto the roof. Together Holmes and I climbed down the pine tree beside the porch and ran across the moon-bleached lawn to the street.

With Holmes in my arms, I slunk down Main Street, keeping to the shadows, wary of every sound. It wasn't the first time I'd sneaked out of the house, but I'd always had Angie with me before. The farthest we'd gone was the soda machine at the gas station, but we'd peeked into plenty of windows on the way, hoping to witness a murder or a robbery. All we'd ever seen, disappointingly, were people watching television or eating or talking on the phone.

What I was doing now was the sort of thing we'd always dreamed of — solving a real, true crime. In some ways I was sorry Angie wasn't with me, but if she were it would be harder to impress her with my heroism. Besides, she'd probably do something dumb and mess the whole thing up. No, I thought, it was best to do this alone.

By the time Holmes and I reached the graveyard, though, I was starting to get scared. Was I really ready for genuine detective work? With one hand on the wrought iron gate, I stared into the darkness. I was tempted to turn around and run back home, and I might have if Holmes hadn't leaped from my shoulder. Slipping between the bars, he paused and looked at me. "Meow?"

He was asking me a question — was I coming? Glancing up and down the street and seeing nothing, I pushed the gate open, flinching at the screeching sound it made, and followed Holmes into Ivy Hill Cemetery.

The moonlight shone brightly on the roadway, casting my shadow ahead of me, inky black, and my feet crunched loudly on the gravel. Thinking I was too visible, I edged off the road into the grass, hoping to hide myself among the tombstones.

As my eyes grew accustomed to the night, I was surprised to see how darkness changed things. The familiar crosses, angels, monuments, and cenotaphs cast strange shadows, and the breeze made a high, sad sound in the treetops. Even the expression on the moon's face seemed different as it peered down from the starry sky.

When I reached the pathway leading to my mother's grave, I hesitated again. The moonlight didn't penetrate the trees shading the old tombstones and mausoleums, and the only sounds were the rustling leaves and the chirping of crickets.

"Holmes," I whispered. "Kitty, kitty, kitty."

He pitter-pattered toward me, his tail aloft, and allowed me to pick him up. Holding him close, I crept down the path. When I reached the place where I'd seen Alice and Clint, I looked around. No sign of anyone. Putting Holmes down again, I shone the light on the old mausoleums lining the path like little houses. Overgrown bushes and weeds hampered my efforts, so I had to work slowly and carefully, checking for trampled grass or broken limbs. To my disappointment, they seemed undisturbed until I got to the last one, almost hidden behind a tall yew tree.

Pushing the branches aside, I shone the flashlight through the bars of the iron gate. Trying not to breathe in the funny smell, a mixture of old basements and damp earth, I stared at the footprints on the dusty floor. Someone had been inside, but where had he hidden the loot?

Checking the gate, I found a loose bar and pushed it aside. Plenty wide enough for someone to squeeze through, I thought. I held my breath and looked behind me, straining to hear the slightest sound. Just crickets chirping, leaves rustling, nothing else.

Then I stepped into the mausoleum. I wasn't sure where the bodies were, but I thought they must be behind the plaques on the walls. Shining the light on the floor, I noticed some of the stones were loose. Scarcely daring to do it, I pried one up and shone the light into the hole, hoping I wasn't going to see a skull grinning at me.

What I saw was a plastic garbage bag. I tried to pull it up, but it was too heavy. The clunking sound it made, though, convinced me it was full of loot. Mrs. Piranesi's antique dolls maybe.

"Meow?" I jumped, and my heart hammered like a machine gun when Holmes brushed against me. Lowering the stone into place, I scooped him up and slipped out of the mausoleum.

"Come on," I whispered, "we'd better go, boy."

But Holmes's body suddenly stiffened. Lashing his tail, he pushed against me with his hind legs. The harder I tried to hold him, the harder he tried to escape. Suddenly he was gone, out of my arms and into the darkness, leaving me standing alone in the tall grass, listening to the crunch of footsteps on gravel.

CHAPTER · 18

Cautiously, I edged into the bushes and crouched down behind my mother's tombstone. My heart was pounding like a drum as the footsteps, two pairs of them, passed my hiding place. I heard them stop a few yards away in front of the mausoleum, but I was pretty sure I was safe.

"Hold the bars aside while I carry the stuff out," Clint whispered, and I felt every hair on my body rise up and quiver. I was right about him. He wasn't just a liar and a big fake — he was also a thief, a criminal, and I could hardly wait to tell the police.

Closing my eyes, I saw my picture on the front page of the *Frederick County Times,* and Clint's too — handcuffed, one arm hiding his face, getting out of a police car. And Alice crying in the background as she went to jail also, as an accessory. They'd be sorry then, both of them, for what they'd done to me!

Cautiously I peered through the branches and saw Alice struggling with the loose bars in the mausoleum gate, her hair and face lit by the glow of a flashlight inside the tomb. While I watched, Clint pulled six black plastic garbage bags out of the hole in the mausoleum floor. One after another, he put them down gently on the path.

"Okay," he whispered to Alice. "Let's start getting this stuff to the van. They're heavy, but I think you can carry one."

Clint hefted a bag to his shoulder and watched Alice struggle to lift one. As they started to walk down the path, though, Clint suddenly stopped. "What was that?" he whispered.

"I didn't hear anything." Alice sounded frightened.

Clint shone his flashlight into the tall grass beside the mausoleum just as Holmes minced out of the weeds, his tail waving. Oh, no, I begged him silently, go back, run, maybe Clint won't recognize you in the dark.

But did Holmes listen? Without a moment's hesitation, the traitor rubbed against Clint's legs, obviously pleased to see him. If my heart hadn't been pounding so loudly, I could probably have heard him purring. Scrunching as small as I could, I cursed myself for having thought Holmes would be a good companion.

Ignoring the circling cat, Clint stabbed the dark with his flashlight. "Madigan," he called, "come here!"

As I watched, too scared to move, Alice grabbed Clint's arm, causing the beam to play crazily over the angels and crosses. "Madigan's not here!" she said. "You don't even know that's Holmes. It could be any old black cat."

"It's Holmes, all right." Pulling away from Alice, Clint started walking toward my hiding place. "Come out here, Madigan," he ordered, and his voice was rough and scary like a stranger's, a criminal's, maybe even a killer's.

Silently I backed away from him, trying to put some space between us. As the flashlight moved closer to me, I stood up and ran. I knew every grave in Ivy Hill, and I thought I could lose Clint if I dodged around enough stones.

"Put out the light!" Alice cried as the beam swung over me. "Somebody might see!"

I heard Clint curse, but he turned off the light as I plunged behind a tombstone into the darkness of an evergreen thicket. With my face pressed against a wreath of flowers, I lay still and listened to Clint moving stealthily from grave to grave. He came very close, then started to walk away from me. Every now and then he clicked the light on, keeping its beam close to the ground as he swept the bushes for signs of me.

"I know you're here, Madigan," he said in his awful new voice. "Stop playing games with me. I won't hurt you, I promise."

"Oh, please," I whispered to a marble angel looming above me. "Please don't let him see me."

But even as I prayed, the light suddenly swung round and shone in my face. In panic, I jumped up and started running again.

"Stay between her and the gate," Clint called to Alice.

As Alice moved to block the path, I doubled back, twisting and turning, scrambling over graves. An angel's stone fingers grazed my cheek, a floral wreath caught at my feet, but I kept going, too scared to call for help. Who would have heard me anyway?

Just when I thought I might get to the street after all, Holmes ran right in front of me and I stumbled. "You stupid cat!" I cried as he leaped out of the way.

Before I could get my balance Clint caught my braid and yanked hard, slamming me backwards against his chest. I felt his arm shoot around me and hold me tight. Then he let go of my braid and clamped his hand over my mouth.

"That's it, Madigan," he hissed in my ear as he walked me ahead of him down the roadway. "I don't know what you're doing here, and I don't have time right now to find out."

"What are you going to do?" Alice caught up with us, her face a white mask in the moonlight. "You aren't going to hurt her, are you?" She sounded as frightened as I felt.

"I'm just going to keep her quiet for a while," Clint said. "I can't let her run home and tell her grandmother, can I?"

At the end of the row of mausoleums, I saw the van

parked where the hearses waited during funerals. Its dull black finish barely reflected the light of the moon.

"Get in," Clint said, keeping his hand over my mouth as he shoved me inside. Pushing me down on the floor, he gagged me with a rag and tied my hands and ankles. Not once did he speak to me or look me in the eye.

When he had finished trussing me up, he sighed. "I'm sorry, Madigan," he muttered, "but I told you to stay out of my private life. Why didn't you listen?"

Still avoiding my eyes, he vaulted out of the van and mumbled something to Alice.

I heard them walk away, their feet crunching on the gravel, but no mater how hard I twisted and struggled, I couldn't free myself. In a few minutes, I heard them coming back with the bags.

"Pile them up around her," Clint said. "Hide her."

After they'd surrounded me with bags, they got into the front seat, and I heard a third voice. Chad's this time. "Mommy?"

"I thought you were fast asleep, sweetie," Alice murmured.

"Hey, son," Clint whispered as the van jolted over bumps, gathering speed.

The tenderness in Clint's voice made my eyes sting with tears. There he was, the father with his son, his true son, the one he'd come back for, riding along with Alice, and here I was, unloved and unwanted, an orphan, bouncing around on a hard floor, feeling every bump in the road. My scalp ached, and the ropes cut into my skin, and I couldn't even tell Clint how much I hated him because of the gag in my mouth.

As we swung hard around a corner, the bags clinking and shifting, I wondered how I could have been so dumb. First, to think a man like Clint, a criminal, was my *father*. Second, to think I could help the police put him in jail. If only I'd stayed home in bed, if only I hadn't brought Holmes with me, if only I'd run faster and hadn't tripped!

Then I remembered the gun. Suppose Clint was planning to take me to some lonely place and shoot me? I'd read a story in the paper once about a girl who disappeared. Months later, some hikers found her body, just bones really, hidden in the woods. She'd been murdered by a stranger passing through town, a drifter like Clint.

Cold shivers ran up and down my arms and legs. Here I was, a poor motherless child, the first person in Frederick County to come face to face with a dangerous armed criminal. What was he going to do to me?

Oh, why hadn't Grandmother listened to Miss Lucas and turned Clint away? She was so smart, she should have known what Clint was. But no — she wanted that hundred dollars a week. She wasn't thinking about my safety — she was thinking about getting the house painted. Well, she was going to be sorry when she woke up and found me gone.

I imagined her calling the police, waiting while they

searched for me. Weeks might go by before they found my body, shot dead.

With tears rolling down my cheeks, I tried to hear what Alice and Clint were saying, but the radio was on, playing bluegrass music, and I could only catch a few words. Then Alice raised her voice.

"What are we going to do with her?" she asked.

Clint mumbled something.

"But kidnapping is serious, Clint!" Alice said loudly. "Aren't we in enough trouble already?"

Mumble, mumble, mumble was all I heard from the mystery man.

Then Alice swore. She knew words I didn't even dare *think*. "We can't take her to — "

Clint turned the radio up even louder, and I couldn't hear another word. The van filled with the sound of Flatt and Scruggs playing "Foggy Mountain Breakdown," and while Chad sang and babbled, I finally fell asleep.

CHAPTER·19

When I woke up, everything hurt. The ropes, the gag, my head. My whole body was stiff and sore, and I was hungry and thirsty. The van wasn't moving, but the bags blocked everything except the sunlight shining in my eyes. I tried to move, but the pain made me groan.

"Are you okay?" Alice leaned over me, her hair tumbling down and tickling my nose.

I looked at her, my eyes filled with tears. How did she expect me to answer with a gag in my mouth?

"Clint's getting us hamburgers and sodas," she said. "He'll untie you when he gets back if you promise you won't shout or run off."

I shook my head, hoping she understood I wouldn't try anything. Chad stared down at me. "Baddy, Baddy! You get up, bad girl!" he chanted.

"She woke up, huh?" Clint's head joined Alice's

and Chad's. He had on his silver sunglasses. "Hold the food," he said to Alice and started the van.

"I thought you were going to untie her so she could eat," Alice said.

"Not here," Clint answered.

The smell of hamburgers and fries made my stomach growl for food, and every bump in the road reverberated through my entire body. Never had I hurt so much, not even when I'd broken my arm falling off my skateboard.

Clint turned the van sharply, jolting me so hard I thought I was going to faint from the pain. He bounced over bump after bump and finally stopped. When he turned off the engine, the only sound was the ping of the motor cooling and the songs of birds.

The seat creaked as he got up and knelt down beside me. "I'm going to take the gag off," he said, "but you better not try anything silly. One yell and I gag you again. Understand?"

Staring at my reflection in his glasses, I nodded slowly. As he removed the gag, I could see the awful red creases it had made from the corners of my mouth across my cheeks. Although I had a lot to say, my jaws were so stiff and my mouth was so dry I couldn't speak.

"Here." He thrust a paper cup at me. "Drink this."

The straw jabbed against my teeth, but as the taste of cherry Coke filled my mouth, stinging my gums, I started crying.

"Oh, come on," Clint said. "You're all right, Madigan. I told you I'm not going to hurt you."

"You won't shoot me?" I croaked.

"Shoot you? Of course not." He looked at me closely. "If you promise to behave, I'll untie your hands," he said.

"I'll be good." I glared at him as he bent over the knots. How could I have ever thought he was my father? He was nothing but a crook, and I was glad I wasn't related to him.

Looking at the welts on my wrists, Clint muttered, "I'm sorry, Madigan. I didn't mean to tie you so tight."

He handed the Coke to me, and I drank the rest of it. "Can you eat?" Clint held out a hamburger and a package of fries and then turned to Alice, who had been feeding Chad.

"See? She's all right," he said.

"I am not!" I glared at him. "You hurt me when you pulled my hair, and I'm sore all over and I want to go home!"

"I can't let you go," Clint said. "Not right now."

"When?"

"Eat your food, Madigan," was all Clint said. Turning his back on me, he got into the front seat and bit into his hamburger.

Unhappily, I nibbled on a cold french fry and tried not to watch Clint kissing Alice. I couldn't decide which one I hated most. They had both deceived me, I thought, and betrayed me. If there were any way I could help the police catch them, I wouldn't hesitate to do it.

"Before we get going, does anybody need to make

a trip to the ladies' room?" Clint looked over the seat at me, and I nodded vigorously.

"You take her," Clint said to Alice.

"But my feet are tied," I said.

Climbing into the back, Clint squatted beside me. "Don't try anything dumb like running away from Alice," he warned me.

"Where would I run to?" I scowled at him as he slowly picked apart the knots. "I don't even know where I am!"

Grabbing me under the arms, he helped me stand up, and it was a good thing he was holding on to me. Otherwise I would have collapsed. My legs and feet were numb, and it took a while to get my circulation going.

"Oh, Clint." Alice looked at him reproachfully, then put her arm around me. "Can you walk a little way into the woods with me, Madigan?"

"Not far," Clint said. "Just behind that big tree." He pointed to a tall oak on the edge of the narrow dirt road. "Don't let her get away from you, Alice. I mean it," he added as she led me into the bushes.

As soon as we were out of Clint's sight, I squatted down and peed as fast as I could, trying not to dribble in my shoes or anything. When I was finished, I asked Alice what they were going to do with me.

While I waited for her to answer, I heard a woodpecker hammering away at a tree. The rich scent of honeysuckle filled the air, mixed with the damp, mulchy smell of the ground.

"I don't know," she said at last. Like Angie, Alice

is not exactly blessed with brains. "Clint's still thinking about it."

"You've kidnapped me, you know. That's a federal offense, much worse than a few burglaries." I glared at her. "When the cops catch you, you'll go to jail for a long time, maybe all your life. Chad will be grown up when you get out, and it serves you right!"

Alice shrugged. "Clint's pretty smart," she said. "He escaped from prison about a month ago, you know. That's why I came back to Hilltop. To wait for him." She paused to watch a butterfly drift past and land lightly in a clump of Queen Anne's lace.

"What was he in jail for?" I could feel sweat pouring off me, soaking my T-shirt, and I had an unreal feeling, like when you're dreaming and you know you're dreaming but you can't wake up.

"Breaking and entering, armed robbery, stuff like that." Alice said this so calmly you'd think she was talking about jobs Clint used to have — fixing cars, installing telephones, working in a gas station.

"At first, I wasn't going to go with him," she added dreamily. "Because of Chad. I didn't want him to know his daddy was a thief." Her voice trailed off and she gazed past me, back at the van where Clint was waiting.

As she ran her hand through her hair, I noticed the rings sparkling on her fingers. "You're crazy to get involved with a person like Clint," I told her. "That whole van is full of stuff he stole. In fact, those rings you're wearing belong to Miss Lucas."

Alice twisted one of the rings and smiled. "Clint

sneaked in her room just before we came to the grave-yard and took them."

Much as I disliked Miss Lucas, the sight of her rings on Alice's fingers made me feel terrible. "She was your fifth-grade teacher, Alice."

"So?" Alice's face lost some of its prettiness as she scowled at me. "She treated me like dirt, and I hated her."

"How about all the other people he stole from?"

"Who in that whole town has been nice to me, Madigan? Mrs. Piranesi? Miss Lucas? Anybody at all?" Alice's voice rose a little. "They've all been awful to me, every single one of them. Even my own parents!"

"What about my grandmother?" Tears filled my eyes. "She never said a single bad word about you!"

Alice's face softened a little. "Clint didn't touch a thing of hers."

"How about *me?*" I screamed at her. "You took me, didn't you?"

"Hey, you two," Clint's voice rang through the trees. "We haven't got all day. Come on."

Without looking at Alice, I ran out of the bushes, back to Clint. He was leaning against the van, holding Chad, bouncing him up and down and laughing the way any ordinary father would.

"Well, you look better, Madigan," he said. "Can I trust you to behave if I leave the gag off?"

Glancing at the silent trees surrounding us, I wondered who would hear me no matter how loud I yelled. "I'll be quiet," I muttered.

"And how about the ropes?"

I shook my head and my braid swung, making my scalp throb a little. "Don't worry. I won't try anything," I said, silently adding "now."

Clint helped me into the back of the van and got in beside me. "You drive for a while, Alice." He handed her the keys. "I drove all night while you slept. I need a nap."

As Alice started the engine, I watched the trees through the windshield. There were no windows in the van itself, so that was the only way I could get a clue as to where we were. In a few minutes, Alice turned left on a paved road and picked up speed, but all I could see was farmland.

We bounced over the country road for at least another ten minutes, and then I felt the van swing around a long curve. In a few seconds, we were on an interstate highway.

Before I had a chance to see a sign, Clint made me lie down again. I guess he didn't want me to know what road we were on.

"The police must be looking for this van by now," I told him. "My grandmother has surely noticed you're gone, and she's smart enough to figure out you have me."

Clint propped himself up on one elbow and shook his head. "I changed the license plates, Madigan," he said. "I'm pretty smart too. And remember, they'll be looking for a man driving — right?"

"Somebody's bound to realize Alice and Chad are mixed up in this." I was thinking of Angie and her suspicions. Maybe she had more brains than I gave her credit for.

"I doubt it. You're the only one who knows about Alice and me."

"How about when she doesn't come to work? Mr. Greene will check up on her."

"Alice told him she was going out of town for a few days to visit some old friends," Clint said.

"Well, they'll catch you somehow," I said. "And when they do, I'll be glad. I hope you rot in jail, Clint James!"

Clint sighed. After a while he said, "Little girls sure are changeable. I used to think you really liked me, but now you act like you hate me."

"For your information, I am *not* a little girl," I said. "And I never liked you, *never!* I've always hated you, right from the start, from the very first time I ever saw you!"

"Oh, Madigan, you don't mean that." Clint gave me one of those smiles that used to make my insides flutter. "You're just mad, that's all."

"I *hate* you." I loaded my voice with ice, wishing I could freeze him solid with the very sound of it. There wasn't a thing he could say or do now to make me change my mind about him.

"You know I really feel bad about this, don't you?" Clint stared at me, his eyes bluer than blue. "I didn't want you to know who I was, and I certainly didn't want to bring you along with Alice and me. Do you think I don't care how you feel or how upset your grandmother must be?"

I hid my face in my arms and refused to look at him. If he thought I was going to believe his lies, he was wrong. I knew who he was now, and I would never forgive him.

I felt his hand on my head, stroking my hair, and, without wanting to, I started crying. "Leave me alone," I sobbed, "just leave me alone!"

I pulled away from him, and the van kept going down the highway, putting miles and miles between me and Hilltop.

CHAPTER · 20

I must have dozed off for a while because the next thing I knew it was late afternoon. Glancing at Clint, I saw that he was still asleep.

Not wanting to wake him, I lay quietly and watched the clouds through the windshield. They were big and white and fluffy, and, as their shapes shifted and changed, I wished I could go back in time to that day at Greenwood Lake. Clint would tell me that he was my father. He wouldn't be a thief but a decent person who was sorry he had left my mother and me. He would want to make up for all the unhappiness he had caused, and he and Grandmother and I would be riding in the front seat of the van right now, going on a vacation or something.

I sighed. That was kid stuff, I thought. Silly daydreams. Clint wasn't my father, he was Chad's father. All the wishes in the world wouldn't change that or the fact that he was a thief.

But still, when I looked at him lying there with his eyes closed, he seemed so innocent. It was hard to believe that he had escaped from jail and robbed houses all over Frederick County. How had he become a burglar? He was so smart and handsome — he could have done anything.

While I was struggling with my own feelings, trying to hate Clint, I heard Chad stir in the front seat. He must have been asleep too.

"Mommy, Mommy, go home," Chad whimpered. "No more car, Mommy."

"What's going on?" Clint asked sleepily as Alice slowed down.

"Couldn't we stop and rest for a while?" she asked, raising her voice above Chad's wail. "I'm really getting tired and hungry, Clint. And so is Chad. He's not used to riding in a car all day."

Clint sat up and looked out the window. "It's almost dark," he said. "Turn off at the next exit, and we'll get some food."

Turning to me, he said apologetically, "I'll have to tie you and gag you again, Madigan."

Since I was hungry too, I cooperated by sticking out my hands and lying still. When Clint had me trussed up and hidden between the bags, he leaned forward to talk to Alice.

"You go in and get the hamburgers this time," he

told her as she pulled off the interstate. "I'll wait here with Madigan and Chad."

Alice parked the van and handed Chad to Clint. "Change his diapers, okay? There's a box of Pampers in the back of the van."

While Clint cleaned Chad up, I lay on my side, my face turned away. I could smell burgers and french fries, and I could hear people ordering food in the drive-in line. It was awful to realize that the normal world was so close yet I couldn't make it aware of me.

In a few minutes, Alice came back to the van with a bag of hamburgers and fries, and she and Clint changed places. He drove for miles down a winding, bumpy road that tossed me around like a sack of potatoes. When we finally stopped, it was dark, and I knew we were way out in the country again. There was no sound anywhere but crickets and frogs and leaves rustling.

Clint untied me and handed me my food. Burgers and fries again and a chocolate shake. "Eat up," he said. "And then we'll be on our way."

After I'd finished, I leaned forward and looked at Clint. He was lying back in his seat, as relaxed and easy as if we were a normal family on vacation.

"How did you get to be such an awful person?" I asked him.

"Me?" Clint widened his eyes like a kid.

"Clint's not awful." Alice leaned across Chad and kissed him. "He's wonderful."

149

"See, Madigan?" Clint turned and winked at me. "Not everybody thinks I'm all bad."

"You're a crook" I said, "and the police are after you."

"They haven't caught me yet, have they?"

"But they will. Crooks always get caught." I stared at him. "In fact, you've already been in jail once. Why do you keep on robbing houses?"

"Somebody once asked Willie Sutton why he robbed banks," Clint said. "You know what he told them?"

I shook my head.

"Because banks are where the money is." Clint put his arm around Alice and hugged her and Chad.

"That's the dumbest thing I ever heard. There are lots of other ways to get money." It made me feel sick at my stomach to see them kissing each other, so I looked past them at the dark trees massed against the starry sky.

"Name some," Clint said.

"Working, getting a job like a normal person."

"Working bores me," Clint said. "And besides, robbing houses is what I'm best at. I have a special talent for it."

"And everybody knows you should use your talent, it even says so in the Bible." Alice started giggling when she said that, and Clint kissed her some more.

"No wonder your parents kicked you out," I said to Alice, but she didn't pay any attention to me. Chad was sitting on her lap, making a mess of himself with the ketchup on his french fries, and she was trying to clean him up.

"Don't you even care what happens to Chad?" I asked Clint.

"What do you mean?"

"Suppose you get in some kind of shoot-out with the cops . . . " I paused, remembering the movie *Bonnie and Clyde*. I'd watched it on television, and it almost made me cry just thinking about the way it ended. What if Clint and Alice died like Bonnie and Clyde? "Or even if you're just sent to jail for a long time. What will happen to Chad?"

"It's not your problem, Madigan," Alice said.

"You should never have let Chad see his father," I told Alice angrily. "He'd have been better off just growing up in Hilltop, not knowing anything about him!"

"Well, you sure have changed your tune," Clint said. "I thought the most important thing in the world was finding your father."

"That's when I thought *you* were my father!" I yelled, hating him again.

"I never meant to mislead you, Madigan," Clint said softly. "I was just so worried that Alice wasn't going to let me see Chad. And there you were, a kid who couldn't remember her father and nobody would tell you anything about him. I was scared Alice was going to pull the same thing on Chad."

"You should have known what I was thinking." Realizing I was about to cry again, I slumped against the bags and tried not to think about the Clint I'd first seen in Sweeney's — the tall, mysterious stranger, his eyes hidden behind his silver sunglasses. That Clint was gone forever. In his place was an escaped convict who'd dragged me away by the hair of my head, and I wasn't going to let him sweet-talk me again. No, sir, not this time.

"I'm sorry, Madigan," he said. "If I did have a daughter, I'd want her to be just like you." Again I felt Clint's hand touch my head, and this time I let it linger there, just for a second, before I jerked away from him.

There was a little silence then. The crickets' voices seemed louder and shriller, and an owl hooted right over my head, sending shivers up and down my spine.

Suddenly, Alice said, "I've got to make a little trip to the ladies' room. How about you, Madigan?"

As I followed Alice into the woods, Clint called after us, "Don't go too far."

Alice led me into a clump of bushes and gripped my arm. "I sure hope you're happy, Madigan," she whispered. "Clint might feel sorry for you, but I don't. You're ruining everything!"

I stared at her face, pale in the moonlight, and wondered why I'd ever thought she was pretty. "You and Clint are the ones ruining things," I said. "Not me."

"It's all your fault for being such a nosy brat. Just because of you, cops all over the country are probably looking for Clint!"

"Well, what do you want me to do about it?" I asked. "I didn't exactly ask you to take me with you."

Alice looked over her shoulder, then turned to me.

"Run," she said. "Get out of here and don't come back!"

"Are you crazy? He'll come after me."

"Just sneak away," Alice hissed, pushing me toward the woods. "I'll stall him as long as I can."

"Won't he be angry with you?" I was so confused I didn't know what to do. Angry as I was at Alice, I didn't want to leave her, not here in the middle of nowhere. She was my safety, Angie's sister. Once she was even my babysitter far, far away in Hilltop.

"I'll worry about that." Alice gave me another shove, harder this time. Her nails were long and sharp and they bit into my skin. "Just head for the woods and run before he catches you. Go on back to Hilltop where you belong!"

"But I don't know where I am, I don't know which way to go." I clung to her, afraid to stay, afraid to go. The woods rose up like a dark wall against the starry sky, and there wasn't a light anywhere. I didn't see a sign of a house or a road, and I was getting cold.

"Will you do what I tell you?" Alice shook me off as if I were a bug. "You're wasting time, Madigan."

"You hate me, don't you?" I whined like a little kid as I backed away from her, scared of the hardness in her eyes and voice.

"Maybe I'm saving your life," Alice whispered. "Have you forgotten the gun?"

"Clint wouldn't shoot me. He promised he wouldn't." My tears blurred Alice's mean-eyed face as I crept away from her, crawling on my hands and knees under the bushes.

"Go on, go on." Alice shooed me the way you'd shoo a stray cat you didn't want around. "Move it, Madigan. I can't stall him forever, you know."

When I reached the edge of the woods, I stood up slowly. My knees felt like water, and I had to hold onto a tree for a second. Dry-mouthed with fear, I looked back at the clearing and saw Clint leaning against the van, whistling "Down in the Valley," just as slow and sad as he'd played it on his harmonica at Greenwood Lake. He held Chad, swaying in rhythm with the tune, pausing now and then to laugh down at his son.

He was as mysterious as ever, I thought, a man of secrets, tall and handsome with moonlight in his hair, and I stared at him long and hard to fix him forever in my memory. I'd never see him again, I was sure of it, and for a moment I wanted to run back to the van and beg him to take me with him. We'd be a family after all, Clint and Chad and Alice and me, traveling across America to places I'd never seen.

As I hesitated, the dark woods at my back, I heard Clint call to Alice, "What's keeping you all?"

"Just a minute, Clint," Alice yelled. "We're doing our best to hurry."

From my hiding place by the tree, I saw her turn and look at me, her face desperate as she signaled to me to run. Glancing back at Clint, I saw him put Chad into the van. Then he started walking toward Alice. Something in his hand gleamed in the moonlight. Scared it was the gun, I crept into the woods.

"What's going on?" Clint's voice carried sharply in the night air. "Did you let her get away?"

He swore, and a flashlight beam chased me through the trees. "Come back here, Madigan!" Clint plunged into the bushes behind me.

Abandoning all attempts to be quiet, I ran, stumbling and crashing into things like a blind person, the flashlight catching at my clothes as I skidded downhill and splashed across a creek. Wet to the knees, I climbed up the bank and kept on running, too scared to think about where I was going.

CHAPTER·21

Once or twice, I thought I heard Clint behind me, but I kept running, despite the pain in my side and the branches whipping my face. Finally I tripped and fell. For a moment, I lay still, trying to get my breath as I listened for Clint. All around me, the woods were silent except for the call of an owl and the sound of the wind in the treetops.

When I was satisfied he was nowhere near, I got back on my feet and started walking, freezing with fear every time I heard the slightest noise. It wasn't just Clint I was scared of now. It was the forest itself — the silent trees in the moonlight, the darkness all around me, the realization that I had no idea where I was or how to get home. I had escaped Clint, for now at least, but I was lost, completely and utterly lost.

At last, too tired to take another step, I sank down

at the foot of a huge oak tree. With my back pressed against its trunk, I listened and watched, straining my eyes and ears for a sign of Clint. Seeing and hearing nothing, I hugged my knees to my chest and shivered. My jeans and shoes were wet from the creek, the ground under me was damp, and the night air was cold. I'd have given anything to be in my own bed with Holmes by my side, purring in my ear.

As I huddled there, all alone, I had a horrible thought. Suppose I starved to death in the forest like "The Babes in the Wood"? My body might never be found, and Grandmother wouldn't know what happened to me. Strangers would see my picture on milk cartons and shake their heads. No, they'd say sadly as they poured milk on their cereal, they hadn't seen me. Then, without another thought, they'd toss the empty carton, picture and all, into the trash.

Oh, why had I gotten myself into this horrible situation? Never again would I try to solve a crime, I promised myself. Never again would I complain about not having anything to do. Angie could chomp her dumb old gum in my ear any old time, Grandmother could give me a million chores, Mr. Schumann could tell me all his jokes ten times in a row, Miss Lucas could go on and on about the rudeness of modern children. If I could just go home, nothing would ever make me angry again.

I must have dozed off thinking about Hilltop because all of a sudden the woods were full of gray early-morning light. My clothes were soaked with dew, and

I was shivering with cold. Gazing around me, I saw nothing but trees rising up into the misty sky. Since I didn't know where the van or the road were, I started walking uphill, trying not to think of people lost in forests and wandering in circles until they died of exposure.

At the top of the hill, I hoped to see a road or a house, a farm maybe, something I could walk toward, but all I saw were trees and the other side of the hill. At the bottom, though, I came to a creek, and I remembered that you should follow water downstream. Sooner or later, you would find your way out of the woods.

It wasn't easy to walk beside the creek. Trees and rocks got in the way, the banks rose and fell, the water widened and narrowed, but I stayed with it, telling myself that at least I wasn't walking in circles. Loops, twists, and turns maybe, but not circles.

I stopped a couple of times. My feet were really blistered, and I was weak from hunger, but I drank the water from the creek, hoping it was clean, and I found wild blackberries to eat.

By afternoon, I was getting more and more discouraged. I didn't want to spend another night in the woods, but I still hadn't seen a sign of a road or a farm. Settling down once more for a rest, I dozed off. The next thing I knew, the setting sun was shooting golden beams through the trees right into my eyes like Clint's flashlight. Startled, I leaped to my feet, ready to run, but the woods were quiet except for a humming noise coming from far away. I sat up and listened to it as it changed into a clattering sound, then turned back to a hum.

"That's a car," I said out loud, "going over a bridge." My voice sounded so strange it scared me. Not just because I was alone in the woods, but also because I was so hoarse I could barely recognize myself.

Sure that I was going the right way, I ran along beside the stream. It was a lot wider now, and when it finally came out of the woods it ran under an old-fashioned wooden bridge with iron sides. I knew Clint hadn't driven across anything like that the night before. I would have been tumbled all over the back of the van if he had.

I stood by a tree for a while, looking at the bridge and thinking. If Clint were still after me, he'd spot me easily walking on the road. Maybe it would be better to wait till dark before I ventured out of the woods. Then every time I saw headlights I could jump off the road and hide.

With hunger gnawing at my insides, I found more berries and ate until it was too dark to see anymore. Then I slipped out of the woods and ran across the bridge, scared to death the van would come bumping up behind me before I reached the other side.

Safely across, I walked for hours with nothing but the moon and an occasional rabbit to keep me company. Three or four cars passed me, but I hid in the tall weeds or bushes, and each one zoomed past without anyone seeing me. I didn't think Clint's van was among them.

Finally I came over a hill and saw the most wonderful sight in the world. A little town, smaller even than Hilltop, was just ahead. And right in its middle was a gas station with a big winged horse on a lit sign. Best of all, a car was parked next to the pumps and a man in coveralls was talking to the driver.

Taking one look over my shoulder at the empty moonlit road, I ran down the hill, my feet throbbing as they struck the hard sidewalk. The man looked up from the car as I tripped and fell almost at his feet.

"Whoa, missy." He helped me up. "Where did you come from?"

For a minute I couldn't speak. I clung to the man, sobbing, breathing in the safe smell of him, gasoline and soap and car grease.

"What's wrong? What's happened?" He held me at arm's length. "Are you hurt?"

The woman at the driver's wheel peered at me, then got out of the car and touched my arm gently. "Can you talk?" she whispered. "Can you tell us your name?"

"Madigan," I whispered, "Madigan Maloney." Then I was crying too hard to say anything else.

Another woman got out of the passenger side of the car. "It's her," she said, "the one we just heard about on TV."

All three of them stared at me. "Please," I wept, "call my grandmother, tell her I'm safe."

"Harold!" the gas station attendant called to someone in the office. "Call the state cops, quick. We've got the girl, the one kidnapped by the escaped convict."

Turning to me, he added, "Come on inside, honey, and sit down. You're safe here, don't worry. Nobody can get you now."

He glanced over his shoulder as if he were making sure, and the two women drew closer to him. Then he took me into his office and sat me down on an old plastic couch already occupied by three skinny cats who ran off in several directions when I joined them. "How about a soda?" he said. "Or a candy bar?"

"Can I call my grandmother?"

I couldn't stop shaking when he led me to the phone, so he had to dial for me. "Mrs. Porter?" he said. "Somebody to speak to you."

Of course I couldn't say a word. I just cried and cried while Grandmother talked to me, trying to figure out what was going on. Finally the man took the receiver and told her I was all right.

"She ran in here, crying her eyes out," he said, "but she's not hurt, just scared." There was a pause. "Why, she's in Ohio, ma'am. About twenty miles north of Columbus."

Another pause. "We're waiting on the police now," he said. "You want to talk to her again, ma'am?"

He handed the receiver back to me and I clutched it, imagining Grandmother at the other end of miles and miles of telephone wire, standing in the hallway of our house, safe and well. On the wall above her hung my school pictures from kindergarten through sixth grade, pictures of my mother, pictures of Grand-mother, and pictures of my relatives and ancestors, going back, back to the time of the Civil War. How I wished I were in that hall with her instead of in this gas station far away from everybody and everything I loved.

"I ran away from him, Grandmother, in the woods, and I was lost for a whole day, and Alice was with him, he's Chad's father, but she helped me get away." The words tumbled out, and then I started crying again. "Can you come get me?" I wept. "I want to go home."

"Yes, Madigan, yes, of course I'll come."

Before she could say anything else, I saw a police car, its lights flashing, pull into the gas station and skid to a stop right in front of me. Two state troopers jumped out and ran toward me.

"The police are here, Grandmother," I said as they entered the gas station and approached me. "I think I have to talk to them."

"Don't hang up," Grandmother said. "I'll need to find out where they're going to take you."

The gas station man took the phone and bent his head to talk to Grandmother as the troopers led me back to the couch and started asking me more questions than I had the energy to answer. They wanted to know if Clint had hurt me in any way, they wanted to know the exact circumstances of my capture, they wanted a description of the van, of Alice, of Chad, of the contents of the van, they wanted to know if I knew where he was going and if I could pinpoint the location of my escape.

By the time they had asked every question they could think of, I was in tears again, so exhausted I wanted to sleep for a year.

Very gently, one of the troopers told me they were going to take me to the hospital in Columbus. "A doctor will check you for injuries," he said kindly, "and you'll spend the night there. Your Grandmother can take you home as soon as she arrives."

While he was telling me this, the other trooper was on the phone explaining it all to Grandmother. "No, ma'am," he was saying, "I don't think she's hurt, but we have to make sure." Then he gave her the address of the hospital and asked her if she'd like to speak to me again.

I took the receiver from him. "When will you be here?" I asked, unable to keep my voice steady.

"It's about a twelve-hour drive, Madigan, so if I leave here at five A.M., I should be in Columbus by dinnertime.

I clutched the phone so tightly my fingers ached. "Is Holmes all right?"

"Holmes? Of course he is. In fact, he's right here beside me." Grandmother sounded puzzled, so I told her about taking Holmes to Ivy Hill.

"I was scared he got lost or something," I said. "Can I say hi to him?"

Grandmother held the receiver to his ear while I said hello. I was sure he said "Meow" before Grandmother got back on the phone.

"You see?" she asked softly. "He's just fine."

"I love you, Grandmother, I love you," I whispered. "And I miss you."

"Oh, Madigan." Grandmother's voice broke into sobs. "Thank the good Lord you're safe. I've been so worried. If anything bad had happened to you, I couldn't have borne it."

Although I didn't want to hang up, the state trooper pried the receiver gently from my hand and told Grandmother the hospital was expecting us. Then he led me out to the car and suggested I lie down in the back seat. "Get some rest, Madigan," he said. "You're safe now."

CHAPTER · 22

All I remember about the hospital is having to answer a lot of questions before they would let me take a shower and go to bed.

They didn't let me sleep late the next day, but they brought me a nice big breakfast, the first decent meal I'd had since I'd left Hilltop. To tell you the truth, I could have eaten seconds and thirds if they'd offered them, I was that hungry.

Then the reporters arrived, asking questions and taking pictures and carrying on as if I were the most famous person in Ohio. TV cameramen filmed me sitting up in bed wearing a dumb little hospital gown and told me I'd be on the national news. It seemed people all over the country had heard about my being kidnapped and were happy I had escaped safe and sound, but somehow it wasn't as exciting as I thought it would be. I kept wondering about Clint — where was he? Would he see me on television?

As soon as the reporters left, one of the state troopers who had brought me to the hospital showed up, wanting to know if I'd remembered any other details. He was particularly interested in Alice.

"I know she helped you escape," Officer Cooper said, "but as far as I can see, she was deliberately aiding and abetting a known fugitive, and that makes her his accomplice." He sounded very official as he told me this, and he didn't smile. Not once. In fact, he sounded so mean and hard he scared me.

Silently I twisted my braid around my finger till it hurt. I thought about Alice flaunting Miss Lucas's rings and saying she hated her and the Piranesis and everybody else in Hilltop, and I remembered despising her for being Clint's girlfriend. In fact, I'd told her myself I hoped she'd go to jail for a long time and never see Chad again.

Now that I was safe, did I really want Alice to be sent to prison? She was my best friend's sister, my old babysitter, Chad's mother. Just a little while ago, I'd thought she was sad and beautiful, a victim of love languishing in Hilltop.

Officer Cooper cleared his throat, and I looked at him. "Whether you want to admit it or not, you were in the company of a dangerous man, an escaped convict, a thief, a kidnapper," he said in his official voice. "When he's caught, we'll need your testimony. I hope you realize that."

Instead of answering, I turned my head and watched the raindrops racing each other down the windowpane. Every terrible thing Officer Cooper said about Clint was true, yet it wasn't the whole truth. It didn't include the way Clint played the harmonica or the things he saw in the clouds or the poetry he knew. It didn't include the way he looked at Chad or played with Holmes or teased me.

How could I stand up in court and testify against him? After all, it was my own fault he'd kidnapped me. What else could he do? If he hadn't taken me with him, I'd have most certainly gone right to the police, but now — well, I wasn't mad any more, and I didn't hate him the way I had.

"Kidnapping is a serious crime," Officer Cooper said, a little louder than necessary.

I hung my head, understanding what Alice meant when she'd said I'd ruined everything. Thanks to me, Clint was in really big trouble.

"And you're lucky to be sitting here safe and sound." He paused and then added in a kinder voice, "Well, I'll let you get some rest, Madigan. You've been through quite an ordeal."

As Officer Cooper's footsteps faded away, I lay back against the raised head of the hospital bed and gazed at the rain falling from the gray sky into the gray puddles on the roof. It was the dreariest view I'd ever seen, and I was glad I wasn't really sick. How could anybody get well if all she had to look at was an ugly, flat roof in the rain?

Turning my back on the window, I curled up in a little ball and wished Holmes were here to keep me company. I didn't want to think about Clint or Alice anymore. I just wanted to forget everything, especially my stupid old daydreams about Clint. How could I have been such a dumb little kid? Believing a total stranger, a criminal, a fugitive, was my long-lost father, and then imagining I could catch a thief all by myself, making one dumb mistake after another. And look where it got me. In a hospital in Columbus, Ohio, scratched all over from briars and brambles and covered with mosquito bites.

Closing my eyes, I tried not to see Clint's face, but he wouldn't go away. Like flashbacks in a movie, I saw him smiling at me, tweaking my braid, playing his harmonica, laughing at Mr. Schumann's jokes. Then suddenly he'd loom up, sinister and dangerous in the graveyard and grab my hair, and I'd remember how it hurt, and how the ropes and gag dug into my skin, and how the van jolted me, and how scared I was in the woods, running, running, running. Wherever Clint was now, did he hope I was safe? Or was he just glad to be rid of me?

Tossing and turning, trying to understand how Clint could have fooled me so, I must have fallen asleep, because when I woke up, even before I opened my eyes, I knew Grandmother was sitting beside me. I could smell old lavender and feel her hand smoothing my hair. I sat up and hugged her hard. "Take me home," I whispered. "Please take me home."

As soon as I was dressed in the nice clean clothes she'd brought, Grandmother checked me out of the hospital and took me to a motel on the outskirts of

Columbus, explaining she was just too tired to drive all the way back to Hilltop.

"We'll leave first thing in the morning, Madigan," she said as I flopped down on one of the big double beds in the room. "Right now, I could do with some dinner and then a good night's sleep, something I haven't had since you disappeared."

"I'll eat anything as long as it isn't burgers and fries," I told her as I followed her happily down the dimly lit hall to the motel restaurant. It was one of those places where there are so many ferns and things you feel like you're in a jungle, but they had a great salad bar and wonderful club sandwiches and the waitress recognized me from the morning news. She made such a fuss over me I got kind of embarrassed, especially when people at other tables started staring at me and whispering.

But Grandmother gave them all one of her best withering stares, and pretty soon they bent their heads over their food and pretended to forget about us.

"Well, Madigan," Grandmother said while we were waiting for dessert (a hot fudge sundae on the house for me). "Perhaps you'd like to tell me what you were doing in the graveyard in the middle of the night."

This was the question I'd been dreading from the moment I spoke to her on the telephone. I knew she'd ask it sooner or later, and I'd been searching for an answer for some time. I began by telling her about seeing Clint and Alice in the graveyard, leaving out the part where I'd flung myself at Clint. It was too embarrassing to admit I'd been so stupid.

"I wanted to be a heroine," I finished. "I wanted my picture in the paper."

"Well, you did become a heroine," Grandmother said, "but I don't think you're enjoying it as much as you thought you would."

I shook my head, and just then the waitress arrived with my sundae and Grandmother's coffee. "Here you are, Madigan Maloney." She set my sundae down with a flourish and lingered for a moment to make sure it was up to my standards. Then she asked me to sign my placemat for her. "I want your autograph," she said as she watched me sign my name in my best handwriting.

"What still shocks me is Clint," Grandmother said after the waitress had left. "I thought he was such a nice young man. It never occurred to me he had anything to do with the burglaries. Marie, of course, is having a field day, boasting to everyone that she knew it all along. It's almost made up for the loss of her rings."

Suddenly she set her cup down, slopping coffee into the saucer. "If only I hadn't rented him that room! This never would have happened if I'd had more sense. The way he quoted poetry and smiled and talked about living with his grandmother — he really took me in. I tell you, Madigan, it makes me feel like a fool."

While I sat there, silently stirring the hot fudge into my vanilla ice cream, she looked at me closely. "What

I can't understand, though, is why you wanted him to be arrested. I thought he'd charmed you, too."

"I was mad at him," I confessed, hoping I wasn't going to cry again, "and I wanted to get even."

"What did Clint do to make you so angry?" Grandmother peered at me over the rim of her coffee cup, waiting for me to go on.

I bent my head over the ruins of my sundae and decided I might as well tell her everything. Knowing her, she'd probably guess the truth sooner or later anyway. "Promise you won't laugh," I whispered.

Grandmother reached across the table and patted my hand. "Of course I won't laugh," she said.

"I know it sounds dumb and babyish," I mumbled, "but I thought Clint was my father, and I was mad when he wasn't. I wanted him to be so badly." Everything in the restaurant blurred, and I rubbed my eyes hard with my fists to keep from crying.

"You thought Clint was your father?" Grandmother sounded surprised. "Good heavens, Madigan, where did you get that idea? If only you'd asked me, I could have told you he wasn't."

"I wanted to talk to you about it," I said, "but I knew you'd get mad. It's easier to ask you about sex than it is to ask you about my father."

Grandmother sipped her coffee thoughtfully, then fiddled with a sugar packet. At last she looked at me. "I didn't realize you cared about your father one way or the other."

"I think about him all the time." I stirred my ice

cream round and round, watching it slowly melt into a thick liquid. "I always have."

"I promised your mother not to talk about him, not to let you see him." Grandmother's voice quivered a little. "I was never sure it was the right thing to do."

"You know something about him, don't you?" I shoved my sundae away, suddenly sick of its sweet taste.

"This isn't the place to talk about it." She picked up the check and examined it. Leaving a couple of dollars for the tip, Grandmother paid the cashier and led me back down the silent carpeted hall to our room.

As I followed her, I walked on one stripe of the carpet, pretending I was balancing on a tightrope. If I fell off, I told myself, Grandmother wouldn't tell me anything, so I held my breath and tried hard not to teeter. I'd waited long enough to learn the truth, I thought, and I reached our door without wavering once.

CHAPTER·23

After we entered our room, I sat down beside Grandmother on one of the double beds. "I really don't know very much about your father," she began. "I never met him, but I do have a picture of him, one your mother sent when she told me she'd married him."

"You have a picture?" I stared at her. "And you never showed it to me?"

"Your mother thought I'd destroyed it, but I saved it, just in case."

"In case of what?"

"In case you wanted to know more about him someday."

"Do you have it with you?"

"It's home in a box of my things. I'll show it to you when we get back." She smiled and stroked my hair. "I'm afraid he isn't nearly as handsome as Clint."

"I don't care if he's the ugliest man alive. I just want to see what he looks like." I snuggled a little closer to her. "What else do you know?"

Instead of answering me, Grandmother stood up and crossed the room to the picture window hidden behind wall-to-wall drapes. Pulling the cord, she opened them to a view of the parking lot and the motel swimming pool. One white towel hung on the fence, and a pigeon perched on the lifeguard's chair. The rain made circles in the water in the pool and in the puddles in the parking lot.

With her back to me, Grandmother sighed. "Oh, Madigan, what's the sense of digging up the past?"

"He's my father, and I want to know about him. Even if it's bad." I followed her to the window just as the pigeon hopped off the chair and flew out of sight. "Even if he's in jail."

"Well, it's nothing that dramatic." Resting a hand on my shoulder, she said, "Meg knew I didn't want her to marry while she was in college, so she didn't tell me until she and Robert were already married."

"That's my father's name? Robert?"

She nodded. "Robert Maloney. He was Meg's first real boyfriend. She was out in California, just starting college, only eighteen years old. He swept her off her feet, I guess." Grandmother paused, her face sad in the gray light coming through the window.

"So she got married kind of young," I said to help her along. "What happened to make her hate him so much?"

Grandmother's breath misted the windowpane.

"Not long after you were born, he left her, Madigan. He just packed his things and walked out."

"Why did he do that? Was I a horrible baby or something?" Although I'd never told Grandmother, I'd always been secretly afraid it was my fault my father left. Maybe he'd been mad I was a girl. Maybe I wasn't pretty enough or I cried too much or got in his way somehow.

"Oh, no, Madigan. It didn't have anything to do with you." Grandmother put her arm around me and drew me close. "You were a darling baby, perfect in every way." She paused again. "He told Meg he'd never really loved her. He'd found somebody else, and that was that."

She gazed at the falling rain. "Meg brought you back to Hilltop, but she never got over him. She was so unhappy, I just can't help blaming him for her death."

I stared at the row of motel windows across the parking lot. Every pair of curtains was drawn except for one. Through the glass, I could see a lamp on a table exactly like the one in our room. I felt as if I were looking into a mirror, with one difference. Nobody stood at the window staring back at me. The room was empty.

"Did he ever try to get in touch with you?" I asked.

"Once," Grandmother said softly. This time she didn't meet my eyes. "After Meg died, he wrote to me."

"Did he want to see me?"
She nodded.

"And you didn't let him."

"I'd promised your mother." Grandmother frowned. "I was worried he might take you away from me."

"Did he say that in the letter? That he wanted me?" I looked at her, alarmed. Here was a possibility I'd never considered.

"He suggested it," Grandmother said unhappily. "He's remarried with a couple of children, and he said maybe he should take you off my hands." She spread her fingers and stared at them. "Off my hands," she repeated, shaking her head. "As if you were a cat or a dog."

"What did you say?"

"I told him Meg didn't want you to have anything to do with him." As she stroked my arm, I watched her hand, seeing the familiar ropelike veins under the skin, the large knuckles, the crooked finger she'd broken as a girl, the thin gold wedding band she always wore.

"Was it just because you'd promised my mother?" I asked, almost afraid to lift my eyes to her face. "Or did you really want me?"

"Oh, Madigan." Grandmother hugged me so tightly I thought my ribs would snap. "How can you even think such a thing? Don't you know how much I love you?"

"Once I heard Miss Lucas tell Mrs. Wilkins you were too old to take on the burden of a child." I leaned against her. "She said you deserved some peace and quiet."

"Peace and quiet?" Grandmother made a snorting sound. "How old does she think I am?" She shook her head.

"Marie Lucas doesn't know anything," she went on. "She's never been married, never had children, let alone grandchildren. Good heavens, Madigan, don't go around eavesdropping if you're going to believe everything you hear."

She gave me another bone-crushing hug. "I would have gladly raised a dozen grandchildren," she said. "I wanted at least four children of my own, but your mother was the only one I had, and I didn't have her nearly as long as I wanted her."

I hugged Grandmother back, and for a few minutes we stood side by side, silently watching the rain and thinking about my mother.

"I guess my biggest mistake was thinking I could be everything to you," Grandmother said after a while. "Mother and father both. I should have realized I couldn't pretend Robert Maloney never existed."

I sighed in agreement. "If he writes to you again, will you tell me?"

"Yes," she said softly. "I think you have a right to know, even to meet him if that's what he wants."

"I would like to meet him," I admitted, "just to see what he's like. But I don't want to live with him. I love you, not him."

As we stood there, I felt all my daydreams about my father the spy, the secret agent, the mystery man fade away. Like the clouds at Greenwood Lake, his shape thinned out and shrank from something fantastic to something small and ordinary, a man who had deserted my mother and me, who had married somebody else, who lived with children he loved more than me. Never again would I imagine him as anything but what he was. Nor would I invent excuses for him. Instead I'd wait for him to tell me his side of the story; I'd listen to it and then I'd decide whether it was true or not.

"It's time for the evening news," Grandmother said, interrupting my thoughts. "Would you like to see yourself?"

Flipping on the big color TV, we watched a breakfast-cereal commercial, one of those happy family scenarios, full of gauzy morning sunshine and smiles. Then the news started, and I was one of the big stories. It was very strange to see myself sitting in the hospital bed, wearing a funny little gown and describing my escape.

It was even stranger, though, to see photographs of Alice, Chad, and Clint on the screen. Alice's and Chad's faces were a little blurry, but Clint's mug shots made him look mean and menacing. If I hadn't known him in real life, I would have thought he was just as dangerous as the newscaster made him out to be.

"What do you think will happen to them?" I asked Grandmother as the newscaster turned his attention to a terrorist bombing in Algeria. "Clint thinks he's too smart to get caught, but I don't see how he's going to get away. Especially now that they know about Alice and Chad."

"Kidnapping you was very foolish," Grandmother said softly. "If he hadn't taken you with him, he could have left Hilltop, and no one would have known who he was or even that he was responsible for the thefts."

"Will I really have to testify against him?"

"Yes, you will." Grandmother said this so firmly I knew she'd never change her mind. "Like it or not, Madigan, Clint is a criminal, an escaped convict, armed and dangerous as the newscaster said. No matter how much you like him, he can't be allowed to go on doing things that endanger the lives of others."

"But he didn't hurt me." My lip started quivering, and I bit it hard to keep myself from crying.

"You don't know what he might have done if you hadn't gotten away. He had a gun, Magidan."

"He could have caught me if he'd really wanted to." As I spoke, I was suddenly sure it was true. Clint had let me go on purpose, he must have.

Grandmother sighed. "Even if he did let you escape, Madigan, you could have fallen and hurt yourself, you could have been hopelessly lost — what would have happened to you then?"

This time I let the tears well up and run down my face. "But he liked me," I whispered, "I know he did. He even said if he had a daughter, he'd want her to be like me."

Grandmother pulled me against her, hugging me. "Of course he liked you, Madigan. But he put himself first, his survival above yours. He left you alone and helpless. It's no thanks to him you're sitting here safe with me."

I leaned against her, too tired to think of anything to say in Clint's defense. It was hard to believe, but not so long ago I'd actually thought it was easy to tell the good guys from the bad guys. Now, the more I learned, the more complicated everything became. Here was Clint, for instance, who cared so much about his son he was willing to risk everything to be with him, and here was my father, Robert Maloney, who cared so little about his daughter he never even really tried to see her.

Yet Clint was the criminal, and my father was just an ordinary citizen. No one was going to send him to jail for what he did to my mother. There was no law against breaking a person's heart and no court on this earth where I could stand up and testify against Robert Maloney.

"Life is so weird," I told Grandmother. "Sometimes I wonder if I understand anything."

"That makes two of us, Madigan." Grandmother gave me one more hug, and then she said, "Let's get in bed and pretend this is our vacation. We can watch old movies till we fall asleep."

And that's just what we did. I saw about five minutes of *The Man Who Knew Too Much,* and then my eyes shut and I let myself sink into the soft mattress, eager for morning and our long drive back home.

THE MAGIC CONTINUES...
WITH
LYNNE REID BANKS

THE SECRET OF THE INDIAN
71040-4/$3.99 U.S.

THE INDIAN IN THE CUPBOARD
60012-9/$3.99 U.S./$4.99 Can.

THE RETURN OF THE INDIAN
70284-3/$3.99 U.S.

I, HOUDINI
70649-0/$3.50 U.S.

THE FAIRY REBEL
70650-4/$2.95 U.S.

THE FARTHEST-AWAY MOUNTAIN
71303-9/$3.50 U.S.

Coming Soon

ONE MORE RIVER
71563-5/$3.99 U.S.